CHEATERS

D0372552

Nan Willard Cappo

Simon Pulse
New York London Toronto Sydney Singapore

First Simon Pulse edition May 2003

Copyright © 2002 by Nan Willard Cappo

SIMON PULSE
An imprint of Simon & Schuster
Children's Publishing Division
1230 Avenue of the Americas
New York, NY 10020

Also available in an Atheneum Books for Young Readers hardcover edition.
Designed by Sonia Chaghatzbanian
The text of this book was set in Cochin.

Printed in the United States of America
4 6 8 10 9 7 5 3

The Library of Congress has cataloged the hardcover edition as follows:
Cappo, Nan Willard.
Cheating lessons / by Nan Willard Cappo. — 1st ed.
p. cm.
Summary: When her team is announced as finalists in the state Classics Bowl contest, Bernadette suspects that cheating may have been involved.
ISBN 0-689-84378-X
[1. Cheating — Fiction. 2. Contests — Fiction. 3. High schools — Fiction. 4. Schools — Fiction.] I. Title.
PZ7.C17374 Ch 2002
[Fic] — dc21   00-140226
ISBN 0-689-86018-8 (Simon Pulse pbk.)

For Ellen and Gradon Willard,
and for Emily

We can do noble acts without ruling earth and sea.

—Aristotle

chapter one

Show me a good loser, and I'll show you a loser.
—Knute Rockne

Bernadette Terrell came home from school and caught her mother snooping in her room.

It was an accidental bust. Bernadette got home at 3:30, her usual time, wolfed down a handful of cookies, then headed upstairs to drop her backpack on her desk the way she did every afternoon. She knew it was her mother's day off because the old Suburban stood in the driveway, and overhead the vacuum cleaner droned.

As she reached the stairs, the roar of the vacuum stopped. Thick carpet deadened her footsteps in the sixteen seconds it took her to climb the stairs and cross the hall to her room, which today smelled faintly of Lemon Pledge. Martha Terrell had her back to the door and was busy reading the application essay Bernadette planned to customize for every college on her list.

Bernadette's eyes narrowed. Her room was always the cleanest in the house, through no choice

1

of hers. She gave her mother five seconds to get more deeply incriminated before she said softly, "I'm home."

Only a guilty person would have screeched like that. Pages scattered as her mother collapsed into the desk chair.

"Bernadette Terrell, are you trying to give me a heart attack?" Martha patted her blouse in the general vicinity of her left breast. "What were you thinking?"

Bernadette let her backpack thud to the floor. "I'm thinking you should stop spying on me."

"I was not *spying,* I was cleaning. If your papers are so terribly confidential you shouldn't leave them lying around in plain sight." Martha abandoned her haughty tone. "You aren't really going to send this, are you?"

"What's wrong with it?"

Martha picked up the pages around her feet. "Well, let's see. 'The entire Pinehurst case was a stinking mess of half-truths and distortions. They gave us a rookie debate judge who thought "negative" was a blood type. She claimed the first affirmative had an appealing speaking manner, but I thought he sounded like a Hitler Youth.'" Martha's eyebrows lifted almost to her hairline. "What's *wrong* with it? It's too harsh, that's what. I'm not saying you shouldn't write about debate—I know you love it, and God knows you're good at it." She flicked a hand at the tops of the bookcases lined with plaques and trophies. "But you're not debating *here*."

Bernadette moved a stack of folded laundry off the bed and sat down. She was one of the five best high school debaters in Michigan. This did not impress her mother, with whom she had yet to win an argument. "Our guidance counselor said we should let our personalities shine through."

Her mother threw up her hands. "Of course! But not your *true* personality. God bless us! *I* know you hate Pinehurst, *I* know you can't stand to lose at anything, but ranting about it on paper isn't very attractive." She pointed a finger at Bernadette. "You catch more flies with a teaspoon of honey than a gallon full of vinegar."

"I don't want flies."

"Colleges, then." Martha leaned forward with her elbows on her knees. "If your own mother won't tell you the truth, who will? And the truth is, sweetheart"—she sighed here, as if a terrible secret were being dragged from her—"you are too critical. Your father and I are worried about it."

Bernadette gave a gasp of part outrage, part grudging admiration at her mother's nerve. *She* was too critical? If that wasn't the pot calling the kettle black, as Martha herself liked to say. And Bernadette's father thought she was perfect—he often told her so.

"You *are*. Of everyone. If a person can't spell

every little word perfectly, or doesn't realize you're quoting poetry—and they better get the poet right if they know what's good for them—you write them off. You treat them like, I don't know what, *servants*—on probation."

Bernadette lay back and pulled her pillow over her head. "I'm not listening," she said into its comforting softness. But her mother's words thumped through like the roar of a distant waterfall.

"People pick up on that. They might not say anything, but they notice. Just look at you this minute. You can dish it out, but you can't take it. And then you wonder why you don't have more friends!"

This stung Bernadette into lifting the pillow. "I don't need a lot of friends. I have Nadine." She wished, as she often did, that life was conducted more like a debate, with flow sheets and rules, timekeepers with stopwatches, and judges who punished illogic with low scores—preferably branded on the losers' foreheads.

"Nadine is like your father and me, honey—she's been your debate partner so long, she overlooks your faults. What if she moves away, or meets some boy? Hmmm? Then where will you be?"

"At Vassar. On full scholarship."

"Not with *this* essay."

There followed a pause so long, Bernadette peeked out from under the pillow. Her mother's eyes were half-closed as she continued reading, and she had her lips pursed up and out in what Bernadette called (to herself) her "contemplative trout" face. Suddenly Martha gasped, and Bernadette braced herself. Her mother had reached the last paragraph. "My greatest accomplishment at this stage of my life will be to beat Pinehurst Academy in debate. They say character comes with defeat. I intend to help Pinehurst develop as much soul-building character as I can."

Martha lowered the paper.

"Mr. Malory says I write with ease and imagination," Bernadette blurted.

"*Does* he." Martha's puckered lips stuck out still farther, as though she did not share the opinion of the best teacher ever hired by Wickham High.

Bernadette sat up and wrapped her arms around her knees. "You *like* Mr. Malory. You told Dad it was high time Wickham got a teacher who would push the kids."

This hit home, she saw. She'd watched her mother at Open House. Martha's skeptical face had said plainer than plain, oh, come on, a handsome, single young man, in a classroom with teenaged girls, what was the principal thinking? and then Mr. Malory came over and shook her hand and commended her on raising such a marvelously questioning student as Bernadette. "She sets the whole room thinking, it's really quite helpful," he'd said, in the upper-class

British accent that reminded Martha, as she confessed later, of Peter O'Toole in *Lawrence of Arabia*, and after that it was all right. Mr. Malory was an O.O.O., one of ours, a Bernadette supporter.

Now Martha said "hmmmm," which was as close as she ever came to admitting Bernadette might have a point, and turned in her chair to study the wall over the desk. Sooner or later everyone did that. Burlap-covered fiberboard stretched from desk to ceiling. Her father had helped Bernadette carry it up from the basement last October. Pushpins impaled more than a hundred three-by-five-inch index cards on an expanse of blue burlap, each containing a single sentence or paragraph printed in meticulous black fine-tip felt pen. It was a quote-board, Bernadette explained, like the one in Mr. Malory's classroom. It hung between ceiling-high bookcases crammed with books, as though the authors had cried out a few of their favorite sentences for special notice.

"We didn't have those in secretarial school," Martha had commented, but not as though she minded, for afterward they heard her on the kitchen phone telling her sister-in-law in Cleveland about it, the pride behind "Did *your* boys ever do anything like that, Cynthia?" as obvious as an elephant to Bernadette and her father, who exchanged knowing smiles.

Suddenly Martha sniffed as though she'd spotted

a quotation she didn't believe for a New York minute. "Speaking of Mr. Malory, why don't you show this essay to him and see what *he* thinks? Since he's so educated and I barely finished high school."

"Maybe I will."

Martha rose to her full height of five feet eleven inches. With the briskness that characterized her movements and her judgments, she briskly wound up the vacuum cleaner cord. "We're having lasagna for dinner," she announced as she trundled the vacuum out into the hall, "and coconut cream pie."

The vacuum thumped down the stairs.

Bernadette's mulish look changed to one of interest. Lasagna and coconut cream pie happened to be what she'd order for her final meal, even if they were the frozen kind. Which these would be. In spite of having received last Christmas the latest edition of *The Fannie Farmer Cookbook* (Bernadette had even sprung for hardback), Martha had not made lasagna from scratch since the last neighborhood wake.

During countless phone calls, when they were not settling the finer points of immigration law for debate or arguing the exact color of Mr. Malory's eyes, Bernadette and Nadine sometimes touched on Bernadette's mother's job. She was the office manager of a family counseling clinic. Nadine insisted that Mrs. Terrell saw so many dysfunctional teenagers all day at work, she probably felt guilty because her own daughter was so beautifully adjusted. No drugs, no pregnancies, no suicide attempts. "Maybe," Bernadette said doubtfully. "But she sure keeps looking. I make president of the National Honor Society and she checks my arms for needle marks."

Now, stretched out on her comforter, Bernadette stared up at the ceiling. Too critical, her foot. Suddenly she scrambled off the bed. From under her desk blotter she slid out a plain white envelope and reverently unfolded a closely typed sheet. Mr. Malory had given her a copy of the college recommendation he'd written. She would not actually mail her first application for four months—she had to wait for her junior grades—but Bernadette believed in thorough preparations.

"Ms. Bernadette Terrell is a quietly tough-minded, intelligent young woman." She liked that: tough-minded.

She could have recited the rest: ". . . work that is consistently superior . . . displays an intellectual curiosity . . . most refreshing. . . ." Ah, here it was: "Both in her writing and her class participation, Ms. Terrell is courteous and fair, though she will criticize in an honest and forthright manner when she feels it is deserved. She sets a high standard for herself and for others—a challenge that will make her a stimulating presence in any classroom."

She sighed happily. Take that, Martha Terrell. Her gaze traveled over the quote-board, and she played the tranquilizing game of letting a random quotation inspire her.

How many loved your moments of glad grace,
And loved your beauty with love false or true;
But one man loved the pilgrim soul in you,
And loved the sorrows of your changing face.

Bernadette read it out loud, but it was her teacher's voice she heard, as though he and not Yeats had written the words — for her. She shivered.

A card on the far edge of the board made her frown, and she clambered onto the desk to see better. That was not her writing. "Before honor comes humility. — Book of Proverbs." Bernadette stared at the firm, nun-taught penmanship, then at the doorway through which the vacuum cleaner had exited. The gall of some people. She unpinned the card and dropped it in the wastebasket.

Paper crumpled. She was kneeling on her college essay. She sat down and considered it one more time. Perhaps the wording *was* a tad strong for debate-impaired admissions officers.

She crossed out "Hitler Youth." In a tough-minded, forthright manner she drew a little caret above it and printed "smug, arrogant rich kid."

She could too take criticism.

chapter two

His mouth is most sweet: yea, he is altogether lovely.
—Song of Solomon, 5:16

Pressed to describe Bernadette Terrell, most people at Wickham High would say: smart. Acute observers might mention the zealot's gleam in her dark eyes, usually veiled by glossy brown hair as she bent over some book; or the poignant but deceptive underfed look of her angular body, which prompted her debate coach to press coupons on her for free sundaes at the Creighton Dairy Belle. Not a babe, Bernadette Terrell, but . . . interesting. Oh, and smart — if you liked smart.

Bernadette adored it. Clever dialogue in movies or books, real wit (not the crude comebacks of the boys on the bus), elegant logic, people who never said "preventative" when they meant "preventive": These were the things that made life worth living.

And this year there was Mr. Malory.

Her mother would be appalled if she knew how much time Bernadette spent dreaming of her teacher's face. She dreamed about the rest of him, too, but the expression Mr. Malory wore while he savored his students' search for the answer was the picture that sweetened her sleep most nights. His greenish-gray eyes would scan each knitted forehead, his upper lip would thin in ever-so-slightly malicious amusement, and the hand not holding the clipboard would ravage his hair into a wiry reddish halo.

Like now.

"Green Team, listen up. In *Wuthering Heights,* Brontë introduces Heathcliff's personality by using a nonhuman image." Mr. Malory took off his reading glasses and slipped them into his sport coat pocket. "What is that image?"

He verified that the two lines of juniors facing each other across the desks in his Advanced Placement English class were paying attention. A smile flitted across his mouth. Oh, she liked his mouth.

"Come on, you loafers. At least pretend you read it." His cultured, resonant, distinctly British voice slayed his girl students and made the boys feel dully American. And rightly so, Bernadette felt. She herself would rather die than muff a book bee question.

Brains were racked and memories probed, but *Wuthering Heights* had been four weeks ago.

Beside her, Nadine scowled behind 400/200 wire rims. The scowl was meant to suggest intense concentration. From long experience as Nadine's debate partner, Bernadette knew it actually meant, "I don't have a clue."

"You get it, Bet." Even in a whisper Nadine's voice came out startlingly deep, at odds with her fragile appearance. She was the only person who called Bernadette by her initials (the "e" stood for Elizabeth).

Bernadette grimaced. She'd gotten the last two.

From her other side came the jingle of heart-shaped earrings. "Heathcliff, Heathcliff. Horse-shit," Lori muttered.

Try "Heathcliff, Heathcliff, he's our man." But Bernadette didn't say it out loud. Lori Besh stood five feet ten inches and had biceps defined by years of cheerleading handstands.

"Eh, you bunch of sissies. Will you let the Blues eat your lead?" Mr. Malory's mocking voice enchanted Bernadette. "Ms. Terrell? Is there more to life than debate?"

She could see the page etched in her mind. But she made her voice tentative. "A pack of dogs?" she asked. "They come in and they're as brutal and unfriendly as their, uh, master?"

People were funny. They could hold a God-given gift like a photographic memory against you. But Frank Malory wasn't so petty. His glinting smile made her stomach muscles tighten pleasurably. Mr.

Malory thought her memory *and* her brains first-rate.

Catcalls and hissing came from the Blues. Her answer put them behind by three points.

"Give me two Hardy novels named for their protagonists," Mr. Malory said.

"*Jude the Obscure* and *Tess of the D'Urbervilles.*" Anthony Cirillo snapped out the answer for the Blues. Figured. It annoyed Bernadette when a good mind was wasted on a jerk. Anthony probably thought it was his acne that kept him dateless, but she had news for him—it was his personality. His job at McDonald's was not the only reason she and Nadine called him "McAss."

He caught her eye and rounded his mouth into a fake "O" of alarm.

Just then Wickham's principal, Mrs. Standish, knocked on the open classroom door. "May I interrupt you, Mr. Malory?" Her face was a mass of fine wrinkles all upturned at the moment in an inquiring smile.

"Absolutely, Mrs. Standish. Always a pleasure." Mr. Malory settled a hip on the edge of his desk and loosened his tie. More than one girlish moan was quickly converted into a cough.

The principal opened her mouth to read from a paper in her hands as David Minor delivered himself of a truly impressive sneeze.

Everyone waited expectantly. Would Mrs.

Standish, a.k.a. Spic 'n' Span, send David to scrub his hands as she often did to students who disturbed the germ-free order of her school? Not today, it appeared. She ignored him.

"Mr. Malory. Class. I've just heard some intriguing news from Dr. Genevieve Fontaine." She gave the first name a French pronunciation, with a soft G, and looked over her paper at them. "Dr. Fontaine chairs the research committee of the National Computing Systems Classics Contest."

Mr. Malory's foot stopped swinging.

"Dr. Fontaine informs me that Pinehurst Academy"—she waited out the usual boos—"finished second in the Classics Contest this year with a score of eighty-five percent. A very good score on so challenging a test, I thought."

More boos. Nobody cared what Pinehurst did.

A bizarre thought occurred to Bernadette, and her glance flew to her teacher. A tiny nerve under Mr. Malory's left eye was jumping. His skin, always pale, gleamed damply paper-white.

"*Wickham* High School," the principal continued, watching Mr. Malory now with arched eyebrows, "received . . . ninety-two percent. The highest score in Michigan!"

She tried to hand Mr. Malory the paper, but he didn't seem to see it. "You're"—he swallowed—"you're certain? They said Wickham?"

Mrs. Standish gave a roguish laugh and stuffed

the paper into his fingers. "Now don't act so shocked, Mr. Malory. Your students might think you didn't expect this of them."

Mr. Malory didn't answer. He was reading.

Nadine shattered the silence with a croaked, "We *won*?"

"We beat Pinehurst?"

"Get out of here!"

"We won!"

"I don't believe it!"

"Oh, I *knew* we could!" That could only be Lori. What a twit. Bernadette's own mother wouldn't have put money on them. Not to beat Pinehurst.

Pandemonium reigned.

Mrs. Standish folded her arms across her chest with all the pride of a coach at the Special Olympics and studied the ten students making the noise of fifty.

Pinehurst students, it had been reported more than once in the *Creighton Courier,* studied to the strains of Mozart. Some of them spoke fluent Mandarin Chinese (and they weren't Chinese). It was an off year when only one Pinehurst senior got into Harvard. This year the Panthers had wiped up the football field with the Warriors 42–6. At home. From sports to academics to faculty credentials, the private school dominated. Even Wickham dropouts knew enough to spit at the Pinehurst name. The only good thing about the place, as far as

Bernadette was concerned, was the hideous purple blazer all its students had to wear. Served them right.

Nadine's fine black hair swung across her glasses as she pounded Bernadette's shoulder. "We beat them! We beat Pinehurst, Bet!"

Bernadette choked. "You know what this means? We're gonna be on TV!"

There was always a televised Classics Bowl matchup between the top two schools in the written Contest. Cable TV, but still. National Computing Systems (NCS), the Detroit-based company that sponsored the contest, promoted it heavily and awarded personal computers as prizes.

Nadine gave a throaty cry. "The Classics Bowl! I forgot!"

"Let's go ask if we're on the team." Personally, Bernadette could not imagine Mr. Malory not choosing them.

They joined the group of chattering students surrounding Mr. Malory, who looked as if he'd just heard Robert Browning's poems had been ghosted by Elizabeth.

"Mr. Malory! Hey! We beat the sissies!" Bernadette greeted him. The principal's thin eyebrows snapped together.

Mr. Malory came out of his reverie. Determination dawned in his eyes. "We sure as damnation did, Bernadette," he said, and earned his own glance from Spic 'n' Span. The use of her first name—her Christian name, he would say—thrilled Bernadette to her socks. He smacked one fist against his palm. "That's nothing to what we'll do in the Bowl. The Wickham Warriors will mow them down like the armies of Macduff."

"'Warriors' is so jock," Lori Besh put in. "Don't you think?"

Bernadette and Nadine exchanged incredulous looks. Lori's dedication to the ancient sport of pom-pon made her one of the biggest jocks in school.

Lori continued. "What about a name that's more, you know, intellectual? Like, I don't know— like 'Wizards'?"

"The Wickham Wizards!"

"Go, Wizards!"

"All right, Lori!"

"Ms. Besh, that's an excellent suggestion. Literary *and* alliterative. Let me see, who *are* our Wizards—"

With a fluttery start of recollection, Mrs. Standish handed him a second sheet.

"It appears that Mr. Anthony Cirillo, you yourself"—he nodded at Lori—"Mr. David Minor, Ms. Nadine Walczak, and"—Mr. Malory glanced at Bernadette's outraged face with amusement—"Ms. Bernadette Terrell were the top scorers on the test. Which makes them the Classics Bowl team. Class, a round of applause for our Wickham Wizards!"

Groans of disappointment from the five not chosen were drowned out by the belch David reserved for special occasions. It rustled the window blinds and relieved them of Mrs. Standish.

"I'll leave you to your fortunate—and, of course, studious—wizards, Mr. Malory. And class—well done. This means so much to everyone at Wickham. The superintendent will be very proud of us." There was a tiny quaver in her voice as, with a little wave, she departed.

Proud of "us"? Bernadette rolled her eyes. As if Spic 'n' Span had had anything to do with it. Mr. Malory grinned at her as though he read her mind, and suddenly she laughed. Oh, so what if the principal wanted to bask in their success. Let her. It would be a welcome change from checking the bathrooms for smokers.

The book bee was abandoned.

"This could be even better than a debate," Bernadette said to Nadine in the general discussion. "It's more about speed and memory than logic. And we've already read a ton of classics this year, and anything we haven't read we can zip through if we skim, so I wouldn't be surprised—"

Nadine put a hand on her shoulder and measured her with calm, dark eyes. "Hey, come up for air. You'd think we just beat Pinehurst or something."

"Sorry." Bernadette blew out a deep breath. "I

still can't believe it. We beat them. We've debated them at least five times and we've *never* beaten them. Is this strange or what?"

"'Strange' is not the word." Nadine's laugh was a delighted guffaw. "It's inconceivable. But so what? You're the one who always says they're not smarter, just richer. We proved your point."

Bernadette did like to say that. It had always seemed a safe enough claim. "Yeah." She smiled widely, forgetting to hide her retainer. "I'll tell my parents they just saved forty thousand dollars. I'm brilliant *without* private school."

Nadine's eyes lit with answering glee. "I'll tell mine it's my Asian genes kicking in." The Walczaks had adopted Nadine as a baby from a Seoul orphanage.

"Watch out. They'll sign you up for Korean lessons."

To her relief, Nadine took the bait and launched into her "I'm Polish-American, I refuse to learn Korean" speech, which was good for at least three minutes.

Bernadette needed the time, because a little voice in her head was trying to ruin her mood. From across the room came another David burp to punctuate the question the pesky voice wanted to know: How could Wickham students possibly have outscored Pinehurst?

chapter three

It's a poor sort of memory that only works backward.
— Lewis Carroll, *Through the Looking-Glass*

Mr. Frank Malory knew more about English literature than anyone still in his twenties had a right to. Though Bernadette preferred murder mysteries (especially Sarah Sloan's) to the novels of D. H. Lawrence, still she could tell that their teacher used only a fraction of his learning to teach her class.

His presence at run-down Wickham seemed a miracle in itself. He was single, everyone knew that. But for someone so personable he didn't seem to have much social life. When LaShonda's Siamese cat had kittens that turned out to be half neighborhood tabby, he took one off her hands. He said it would give him someone around his flat to talk to.

Back in October, Bernadette had asked him to act as a judge at Wickham's own debate tournament.

Mr. Malory hesitated. "I don't know the topic," he said. "You might as well ask the custodian."

"It's U.S. immigration policy," she said. "You *are* an immigrant, aren't you?" Oops. She'd made it sound like he swam to Ellis Island. "I mean, you're not American."

He laughed. "Hardly. But there are in-betweens. Do you know what a nonimmigrant visa is?"

He hadn't known her long. She forgave him. "A temporary visitor's pass, as opposed to a green card that gives an alien permanent resident status. Let's see, this is your second year here, you're an English teacher, which means you can't have needed a Labor Certification, so your visa is probably a J-1, for some kind of exchange program. Am I right?"

He gave her a long, quizzical look. "J-1 it is. Unless I apply for a green card, of course."

His tone was joking, but Bernadette answered him seriously. "You could do that," she conceded. "But the immigration people won't like it. They'll figure you planned to do that all along."

"Only if I had applied within the first few months I was here, is what *I* heard. Where do you get your information?"

"Debate research. Wickham has a very strong evidence squad."

"So I see." His mobile mouth twisted in a grin that drew an answering smile from her. "All right, then. I suppose I could judge a round or two in not quite total ignorance. Where and when?"

Truly, a good sport.

He seemed quite happy in America, sometimes dismayed but more often amused by his woefully underread students. Bernadette decided he was biding his time until greater things came along. And they would, she felt sure, if there was any justice in the world.

He could challenge her favorite opinions in the nicest way. Back in November they'd covered *The Great Gatsby*. Bernadette did not approve of books where married people slept with people they were not married to. She said so.

"That's rather sweeping, don't you think, Ms. Terrell?" Mr. Malory had asked. "In this day and age?"

"If it's wrong, it's wrong," she said. "The day and age shouldn't matter."

Mr. Malory was rarely at a loss, but this surprised a small laugh from him. "One reason we read novels is to decide for ourselves whether a breaking of social conventions may not represent a higher individual morality. You've read *Huckleberry Finn*, I take it?" Bernadette had seen the movie. She nodded. "Huck flouted the convention of slavery. Was he immoral?"

A smart debater did not get tricked into conceding an analogous point. Slavery was not the issue here. "Are you saying adultery is a higher morality?" Bernadette asked.

He laughed. "No, I am not. I'm saying it's provincial to cut yourself off from excellent books because you think you know what they'll say. Good fiction isn't comfortable all the time. We need to decide firsthand whether characters have done the right thing. Or if, indeed, there *is* a right thing."

"There's always a right thing," Bernadette said firmly. Provincial, her foot.

He smiled as though he found her quaintly delightful. "And may you always find the courage to do it, Ms. Terrell."

He had eyes the greenish-gray of Lake Erie after a storm. And a nose like a Greek statue. His smile soothed her ruffled feelings, and Bernadette contentedly let the discussion move away without her. All right. She would be more tolerant of books about bums. She would consider their circumstances, read what they had to say for themselves—and *then* hope they got killed off in the end.

Mrs. Standish broke the news of Wickham's victory to the whole school during fifth-period announcements. In biology, Mr. Fodor forgot to be annoyed at being robbed of precious class time long enough to exclaim, "All right!"

Cheers echoed up and down the halls. The win could have been in Norwegian thumb-wrestling for all anyone cared. Wickham had slain the giant.

A girl wearing jeans dangerously low on her hips stopped Bernadette during change of class.

"You're in that advanced English class, aren't you."
She fingered a gold ring in her navel. "I hope you
beat the crap out of Pinehurst. That place really
pisses me off."

"Oh. Well . . . thank you very much." Bemused,
Bernadette watched her slouch away. Plenty of kids
at Wickham had pierced body parts, haircuts she
herself would sue over, tattoos they would live to
regret. Usually she paid them no attention. They
didn't strike her as readers. But now she grinned,
absurdly pleased. She had a groupie.

In study hall she pulled out her notebook.
According to a film they'd seen once in art class,
there were at least seven kinds of intelligence.
Watching, Bernadette had mourned briefly for the
kinds she didn't have: She would never play her
violin at Carnegie Hall, never be asked to paint a
mural in a Detroit museum, never be on the Nobel
short list for brokering peace between Israel and
Palestine. She cheered up when the film moved on
to what she *was* good at: taking tests. Her mental
skills shone on word puzzles, quiz shows, essay
questions—anything requiring memory (though
her logic was pretty good, too). If asked—Nadine
was the only one who ever asked—she could recite
all Jane Austen's novels in the order they were
written; how many Balkan refugees had received
immigrant status since 1995 (*Newsweek* and *Time*
offered different figures); and the titles, in

sequence, on the *Reader's Digest Condensed Books* in her parents' living room.

So it shouldn't be hard to recall test questions from five weeks ago. She jotted down all the names she remembered. Sophocles and Aeschylus. *Canterbury Tales.* O'Neill's *Desire Under the Elms.* Eliot and Dickens and Twain and the other Eliot and more. National Computing Systems might be a bunch of techno-nerds, but they had high literary expectations for today's youth.

So far, she had remembered (with the help of the list on the back of a Cliff's Notes) about seventy-five titles or authors from the test. Of those, she had recognized about half. Still, after listening to Mr. Malory all year, she'd made far better guesses than she could have made the year before.

Assuming a generous hit rate on the guesses, her own score *might* have been as high as 90. Or 85. It *was* a hard test, as Spic 'n' Span had pointed out. Lori Besh must have been flipping coins.

A little worm of dread quivered far down in her belly. For five students to average ninety-two percent, some of them must have scored close to perfect.

Perfect scores. On books they'd never read?

She told her mother the news in the kitchen after school. Martha splattered chocolate pudding all over the frozen pie shell she was filling.

"Bernadette! At least you've ruined your eyes for *something*. I'll bet your teacher was thrilled."

"Dumbfounded."

"No wonder. Beating out Pinehurst!" Some of the most disturbed teenagers at Martha's counseling clinic attended private school, a statistic she mentioned whenever they drove past an especially well-groomed campus. "I always said those people had more money than brains. Wait'll I tell your Aunt Cynthia. She sent your cousins to that expensive Lutheran school, and I never heard of *them* going to any Classics Bowl."

"It's a Michigan contest, Mom. They don't have it in Cleveland."

Martha waved off such irrelevance as she handed the pudding beaters to Bernadette. "I've had my doubts about your Mr. Malory," she continued. "I thought, heavens to Betsy, might as well put a cat in charge of the parakeets. But any teacher who can get you kids into the Classics Bowl is doing something right." She licked the spatula with an absent expression. "We thought of sending you to Pinehurst once."

"*What?* Get out. I never knew that." Bernadette stared at her mother. "Why didn't you?"

"Money. But then someone at work said they knew someone who went there on scholarship, and I thought, well, there aren't many kids smarter than my Bernadette, so I checked it out." Martha's laugh was bitter. "Pinehurst was shocked to hear such a nasty rumor—wanted to know who'd told me. Said it cost more than nine thousand dollars a year no matter how smart you were. Or how stupid, I guess." She laughed again, but her eyes never left Bernadette's face.

Bernadette felt the silent question there. She licked chocolate from her thumb. "If I'd gone to Pinehurst, I'd have never met Nadine." She shrugged. "And anyway, I look terrible in purple."

Her mother said "hmmm" in a noncommittal way. But Bernadette had given the right answer, she could tell.

Joe Terrell's pleasure showed in his voice. "Good job, pumpkin." Her father set down his suitcase and wrapped her in a bear hug.

"Jeez," Bernadette said into his suit jacket. His reaction surprised her; she brought home academic honors on a fairly regular basis. "I haven't gotten this much attention since I ate your boss's pie at that picnic."

"The Classics Bowl is a big deal."

"It's only cable, Dad. Nobody watches it."

"Every agent in the Southfield office will watch it or I'll know the reason why. The NCS Classics Bowl! Their headquarters is right across from my building, you know." Bernadette knew. "This'll look good on your applications, kiddo. Especially if you win."

Her father had lost his job four years earlier when half his firm's workforce had been "downsized" into unemployment. In the eighteen months he'd been out of work they'd spent most of her college fund.

"Bernadette and Nadine are both on the Bowl team," Martha informed him. "If the other kids read half as much as those two, Wickham is in like Flynn." She handed three plates to Bernadette to set on the table.

"Oh, we're in." Bernadette thought of Lori. "I don't know about Flynn."

Martha turned from the stove to stare at her in accusation. "This *is* Pinehurst, am I right? Didn't I read something about you wanting to help them build character through defeat?"

Bernadette didn't answer. Sure, but . . .

Her mother sized her up as though she were a new client with dubious HMO insurance. "You can't wear your hair like that on TV. It's as limp as this dishcloth."

"Eh. They don't give points for hair, Martha." Joe Terrell smacked Bernadette on the bottom with his rolled-up *Wall Street Journal.* "She'll look great on TV, giving 'em hell."

Bernadette's smile was forced. She wished she could be as confident as her parents. Her delight at this morning's announcement had slid, by degrees, from amazement into doubt, and at this moment teetered just this side of disbelief. What if there'd been a mistake? If she could just know for *certain* that the Wickham Wizards *deserved* their win—that it was a genuine, true win, no mistakes—she'd phone Aunt Cynthia herself.

chapter four

Some people built castles in the air. She constructed hers
from mashed potatoes, which kept down demolition costs.
 —Sarah Sloane, *Borrowing Privileges*

That was Monday. Tuesday at lunch, Nadine produced a clipping about the Classics Bowl from the
Detroit Free Press.

Bernadette had expected coverage in the
Creighton Courier (The Latest News About Your
Life and Car). But the *Free Press* was big time.

"Yeah, look, it's all about Phoebe Hamilton and
how she started the Classics Bowl. They list our
names. *And* Pinehurst's." Venom crept into Nadine's
froggy voice.

"So?"

"So—Glenn Kim's on it. Uriah Heep, remember?" Nadine's black eyes gleamed. Glenn Kim was
the second affirmative on the debate team that had
beaten them in January. Two affirmative speakers
set the terms in a debate round. The written case
they presented in the first eight minutes was what
the negative side then tried to tear to shreds. While
Bernadette and Nadine had developed two different

cases they could defend at any time, their preference was to attack. "What I wouldn't give to humiliate him. You can tell he's really Korean. Probably grew *up* speaking it, and how tough is that?"

Bernadette didn't think it such a hanging offense. But she was happy to foster this animosity. If Nadine had a teensy flaw, it was that she sometimes lacked the killer instinct. "A piece of cake. Anyone could do it."

"You're not going to like this," Nadine said, and lowered her voice as if to reveal a dark secret, "but one time I heard him say something to his partner about . . . Twinkies."

Bernadette studied Nadine in some perplexity. Then her mouth dropped open in fury. "He called us *Twinkies*? You mean as in cupcakes? Bimbos? Why, that conceited horse's—"

"Not *us*. *Me*. A Twinkie is yellow on the outside, white on the inside. An Asian who thinks she's white. Get it?"

"Oh." Bernadette never thought of Nadine as Asian. She was not convinced. "Maybe he was just telling the blond guy what he brought for lunch."

"Nope. It was a slam. I've heard it before."

"Well, good. Fine. All the more reason to annihilate him in the Bowl. Not to mention that he looks like his underwear is monogrammed."

Nadine chuckled and slid the clipping across the table.

They'd made the Suburban News section. In a boxed aside, the paper had printed Mrs. Hamilton's response to a question from a recent Business Education Forum. A teacher had asked whether the difficult Classics Contest and Bowl questions didn't pose a risk of injuring student self-esteem.

Mrs. Hamilton had replied: "Self-esteem is a by-product, not a goal. If we fail to introduce our children to what the best minds through the ages have found wise and true, they will leave school barely able to grunt but feeling good about it. Instead of whining about the rigor of the test, teachers should be held financially responsible for their students' performance on it."

They'd printed her picture. White hair stuck out from her head as she stood staunch against the winds of academic laziness.

Bernadette whistled. "I bet that teacher *crawled* out of there."

"Crying," Nadine agreed. She waved at someone over Bernadette's shoulder. "Don't look now, but Lori Besh is coming this way."

"Is this seat taken?" Lori balanced her tray on one palm.

"Ralph Fiennes is joining us, but you can sit here till he comes," Bernadette said.

Lori slipped out of her letter jacket. *"Wickham"* was emblazoned on the back in white on dark green.

It might have been designed to set off her auburn hair. She slid into her seat. "Oh, I love him. I've seen *The English Patient* four times."

So had Bernadette. (Extramarital romance was surprisingly easy to watch when the male lead made your bones melt—and besides, the lovers died in the end.) She regarded Lori with more interest.

Today little metallic fish swung from her ears. The left fish dangled beside a tiny silver ring and a plain diamond stud. From her strong, slender fingers ending in silver-flecked polish to the reddish hair pushed casually behind her ears, Lori projected an easy, Amazonian elegance.

Even her food was camera-ready. Her tray held a bowl of canned peaches, carrot sticks in a paper cup, and a dish of steaming acorn squash flanked by two glasses of orange juice.

She saw Bernadette staring. "Orange Day," she explained. "If I only eat certain colors it helps me keep the calories down. You know?"

"Absolutely," Bernadette replied. "I do that, too." She dumped cherry Jell-O onto her mashed potatoes and stirred in just a pinch of mushroom meat-loaf gravy. "Like, today is Puce Day. You know?"

Nadine winced.

"That's gross, Bernadette. Sometimes I can't believe you're so brainy," Lori said.

Bernadette arched an eyebrow Malory-style. "What do you care about my brains, Lori?"

"You're a *Wizard* now. I want us to win. You think we can, don't you?"

Her earnestness made Bernadette squirm. "Why not?"

"Good. Because I just canceled out of the Governor's All-Star Pompon Competition. Turns out it's the same Sunday. But I don't care—I'd rather be a Wizard."

Nadine looked suitably impressed. Bernadette arranged her own features into insincere admiration. "Well," she began, "I for one am grateful for it. Cheerleading's loss—"

"Pompon," Lori corrected.

"—sorry, *pom*pon's loss is the Wizards' gain. How would we handle those tough questions on literary gymnasts through the ages—ow!" Nadine's kick almost broke her ankle.

"Hey, did I tell you what my dad said about Spic 'n' Span?" Nadine asked. Mr. Walczak was on the school board. "This Classics Bowl thing puts her in the running for a Lifetime Achievement Bonus. The board gave seven thousand dollars to the last principal. And Standish retires in June."

"If they're giving out bonuses they should give one to Mr. Malory." Lori pulverized a chunk of carrot between small white teeth. "*He's* the miracle worker. I love how he'll say stuff in Latin and then go, 'As you all know.' Yeah, right. Like we *know*," she crowed. "I love that."

Bernadette loved that, too. It was one of her favorite things about him.

"I always feel like I'm watching PBS in his class. It's not like he's really *handsome*," Lori went on, "but he's *attractive*."

"Anthony says he's probably gay." Nadine sent a sly look toward Bernadette.

Bernadette gasped. "What Anthony Cirillo knows about sex would fit in a pinhole with room left over," she snapped. "And Mr. Malory even let him drive his Porsche around the parking lot! Anthony is a creep."

Nadine's deep laugh drew glances from other tables. "Bernadette's got a thing for Malory," she told Lori.

"I respect his mind," Bernadette said stiffly.

"*I* think he's drop-dead sexy, not that he'd care. You can tell he'd only go for someone supersmart." Lori sipped her juice.

Bernadette was smart.

"Someone who'd rather read than eat," Lori continued.

Bernadette looked at the gray mound on her tray. She'd much rather read than eat that.

"Probably someone incredibly built," Lori said blandly. "Like, say, a college professor who models lingerie part-time."

She smiled sweetly and let her eyes stray briefly to Bernadette's sweater, which would have fit the same on a ninth-grade boy.

Bernadette looked back with wary respect. "Have you ever read *Prometheus Bound*?"

"Hmmm—nope, must have missed that one," said Lori, with an amused look at Nadine.

"Me too." Nadine had the same faithful note of amusement in her voice.

"Death Comes for the Archbishop?"

They shook their heads.

"Bleak House? MacBeth?" Bernadette persisted.

"I just finished *Don't Open the Door.* About this girl whose stepfather, you know, uh, abuses her?" Lori gave a questioning little pause. "At the end she shoots him. And in the sequel she turns into a drug addict from all the pressure. I can't wait to get it."

Bernadette counted the fluorescent light strips on the ceiling.

Nadine rushed in. "I liked *No Tears for Karen,* where this girl gets cancer. You know?" She might have been Lori's clone. "Her boyfriend drops her, and even her best friend won't go to the mall with her because she's bald."

"Bald! That would be the worst." Lori shuddered.

"You guys." Bernadette balanced a spoonful of puce potatoes on the rim of her plate. "I'm talking about *real* books. Like *Anna Karénina,* which you raved about for weeks and don't pretend you didn't."

Nadine hesitated. "I did like it." To Lori she said, "It's by Tolstoy. Do you know it?" Bernadette snorted, but Nadine ignored her. "This woman, Anna, has a darling little boy and a pretty good husband—for back then, anyway—only she falls in love with this soldier and they have an affair, which is a huge scandal, and she gets kicked out of all decent Russian society."

Lori's blue eyes brightened. "That's just like *Hope Springs Eternal*!" she cried. "It's on right after school. Alicia has a three-year-old named Corey, who everybody thinks is her husband Blake's son but he really isn't, and then she falls in love with Kenyon! Only he's not a soldier. He's a pediatric neurosurgeon." In the silence at the table she drained the second orange juice. "I didn't know Tolstoy wrote stuff like that. I mean, you hear *War and Peace* and you figure, boring. Maybe this Classics Bowl won't be so gruesome after all. I'm lucky at tests, but still—" She seemed to debate whether to address Bernadette or Nadine, or even to speak at all. She went with Nadine. "I really, *really* want us to win. I have pompon trophies all over my room. But I never won anything for being smart. You know? Not even a spelling bee." She smiled wistfully. "My mother would flip. She says I'm a true space cadet."

"What does your father think?" Bernadette asked, remembering her own parents' pleasure.

Lori's face froze. "Nothing. He's dead." Her voice had gone tight and brittle.

"Sorry," Bernadette mumbled. She had been crushing a packet of saltines with her spoon and now she tilted her head back to pour cracker crumbs into her mouth in noisy embarrassment.

"Don't be. Even if he wasn't, he wouldn't care about this stuff." But all animation had vanished from Lori's face, and for an instant she looked like a different person. She looked—bleak, Bernadette thought. Lori slipped her purse strap over her shoulder and stood up. "Anyway, you gotta admit," she said in her normal, cheerful voice, "it would be cool to win. See you."

Along with the cafeteria's male population they watched her carry her tray to the assembly belt. Her lithe figure moved the way Bernadette imagined Cleopatra had walked among her subjects.

"I like her." Nadine took a long, thoughtful sip from her Diet Pepsi. "As for you—way to go, Miss Congeniality."

"Excuse me for not sucking up like *some* people."

"Being pleasant is not sucking up."

Bernadette made a pfffft noise. "'Orange Day.' Come on. And you never read *No Tears for Karen.*" Her clumsiness about Lori's father still troubled her, and made her tone sharp.

"So what? I could have. It didn't sound any dumber than *Look Under 'C' for Corpse*."

"Sarah Sloan books might raise Lori Besh's IQ to triple digits."

"She can't be too dumb if she scored in the top five. Besides, to get in Malory's class you had to be recommended."

"She has two outstanding recommendations." Bernadette cupped her hands in front of her chest.

"She can't help how she looks."

Bernadette's reply would have earned them a sportsmanship penalty from any debate judge. "She can help being a twit. She reminds me of that awful Jillian person in eighth grade."

Nadine's quick grin showed that she remembered very well how she had first met Bernadette.

After Joe Terrell lost his job, Bernadette had transferred out of Catholic school. She started eighth grade at North Creighton Middle School not knowing a single person. She was well aware of what happened when you ate lunch alone for too long—you became a loser, someone with no friends. She didn't know the precise amount of time involved before the "loser" label became permanent, but she gave herself one month.

She tried hard. She smiled whenever she caught someone's eye. Laughed at any jokes she heard. Sometimes after she spoke up in class—she loved to speak up in class—she thought she heard snickers.

Was there something ridiculous about her—her appearance? her voice?—that her friends and family had never mentioned? She couldn't ask her parents—they felt guilty enough at making her switch schools. She would have asked her old friends but, as several of them told her on the phone, eighth grade was keeping them swamped. She heard this with an envy so violent, it scared her. It certainly kept her from admitting that she had to double-check her algebra and rewrite perfect drafts just to stay occupied until dinner.

She'd been in school three weeks when a chance came. At lunch Bernadette was pretending to be absorbed in a dog-eared copy of *The Fellowship of the Ring* when someone sat down across from her. Jillian something, from American History, a gleaming-haired girl always chatting and giggling with coed clusters of friends.

"Hi," Bernadette said. No response. "My name's Bernadette."

The girl lifted her eyes just as high as the chocolate stain on Bernadette's T-shirt, which Bernadette had decided that morning was so faint as to be unnoticeable. Jillian's curled lip said clearly this was not the case. "Hi," she finally said, as if it cost her money.

This must be God punishing her, Bernadette realized, though for what she didn't know. She would try harder. In breathy tones she said,

"Didn't you just *love* the way Mrs. Pruitt talked about the Boston Massacre? It was like, wow, I could really imagine being there."

Yes! Jillian was putting down her soda! Making eye contact! "There was a massacre in Boston? Like what—a sniper or something? And you *liked* it? You're sick." She picked up her tray and flounced away to squeeze in at the crowded center table where a seat had opened up.

Bernadette's cheeks flamed as she scanned the room for lethal weapons. Her old school had featured heavy metal crucifixes with nice sharp edges—in a pinch she could have slit her wrists. But the most dangerous thing she could see in this godforsaken place was the plastic spoon-fork on her tray. *Could* you commit suicide with a spork?

Suppressed giggles exploded nearby. Two girls at the end of her table were holding their hands over their mouths.

The black-haired one said kindly, in a croaky voice, "You gotta understand—all the easy-readers on the Boston Massacre were checked out."

"Wait'll she looks for it on the news at eleven," the other girl said, and stifled a shriek of laughter.

"My name's Nadine," said the frog-voiced girl. "Is that as good as *The Hobbit*?"

"What?" Bernadette stared at the book on her tray. "Oh—it's better." She snapped it shut and slid it down the table like an offering. For the first time in weeks, she returned a smile meant for her. "Here. You read it and tell me what you think."

The rest had been history—and English, and math, and sleepovers, and countless Saturdays of debate. . . .

Now Nadine was groaning in recollection. "Jillian! What a little twerp she was! Not to mention dumb as a stone." She frowned across the table. "But Bet—Lori's not like her. Lori's good-looking, I know, and maybe no nuclear physicist. But Jillian was *mean.*" She glared at Bernadette as though she could implant this essential distinction into her friend's head by force of will. "You can't let ancient history screw up your logic. Lori is okay."

Bernadette scrutinized her plate, pretending deafness. Nadine was right, of course. Why was that so hard to admit? "All right. I'll behave myself, I promise." People with only one friend to eat lunch with should be careful. She thought of her mother's advice—was *this* what Martha meant about being too critical?

"All right, then." Nadine twirled a french fry in blueberry yogurt before eating it. *"Prometheus Bound!"* She shook her head. "Gimme a break."

"It was on the test. I wrote down all the questions I remembered."

That caught Nadine's interest. Bernadette

thought it would. "I can't remember any of them. What else was on there?"

"*King Lear.* Kafka's *Metamorphosis.* Euripides."

"I knew *King Lear.*" The absorbed voice belonged to bookish, competitive Nadine again. "I guessed on Kafka."

"Me too."

Nadine ate another blue fry. "It *was* a hard test." She peered through her bangs at Bernadette.

"Very."

"Of course when Malory teaches a book, you remember it."

"When he *teaches* it, yes. You do."

"He's a great teacher."

Bernadette remained silent.

"And slim-hipped," Nadine added.

"What do his hips have to do with anything?"

"I'm just changing the subject. I'm tired of obsessing about the test questions, if you really want to know."

"I'm not obsessing!" Bernadette said. Nadine raised an eyebrow. "All right, maybe I am. But Nadine—tell me you really think David Minor got a ninety-two percent. There were books about *girls* on that test. Fully clothed."

"What's your point? Are you saying somebody cheated?"

"No!" Bernadette hesitated. But wasn't she?

"Three teachers proctored it. Mr. Malory opened the test right there in the classroom, sealed and everything."

The NCS tests were delivered registered mail and not opened until the test date. Wickham had paid $250 in entry fees to compete. Mr. Malory had hoped this information would make them seriously try on a test that did not, after all, affect their GPA. "He handed the tests to Ms. Kestenberg when the time was up," Nadine added in a "so there" voice.

Bernadette would trust their debate coach with her darkest secrets, if she had any, so she felt ridiculous as she muttered, "She took them down to the office *alone*."

"So?"

"The school that wins the Classics Bowl gets laptop computers for the coach and team members," Bernadette said. "And each kid gets a ten thousand-dollar scholarship to whatever college they're going to."

Nadine stopped stirring her drink. "Ten thousand dollars? *And* a laptop? That's terrific. Are they made of money? Ms. K. was just saying on Saturday she was saving for a laptop. Are you sure about that?"

"It's their Tenth Anniversary Bowl. That's why it's so much. It was in the brochure at the office." Bernadette grabbed the news article. "Here it is at the bottom."

Nadine pushed the article away. "Ms. Kestenberg is a *teacher*. And she's not even the coach. Oh, wait— maybe you think Mr. *Malory's* in on it. Maybe he promised to hand his computer over after we win." Her taunting voice lashed Bernadette. "If anyone cheated, then we're not the real winners and we'll go on TV against Pinehurst and look like dopes." She got up. "You think too much. What you're saying is libel."

"Slander."

"Whatever. It stinks." Nadine picked up her tray. "And you have crumbs all over your face." She marched to the conveyor belt and slid her tray down the line so hard, it banged into another tray and broke a glass. An angry "Hey!" came from behind the kitchen wall.

Bernadette's lips pursed into a modified trout face. With dignity she brushed off her cheeks. With her fork she made precise crisscross tracks in the puce-colored glop on her plate.

You shouldn't let emotion screw up your logic. If Nadine had stuck around, it would have been Bernadette's turn to point that out.

chapter five

The spirits that I summoned up / I now can't rid myself of.
— Goethe, *The Sorcerer's Apprentice*

It took all of fifth period for Bernadette to reach the conclusion that possibly Nadine had a point. Again. Possibly she, Bernadette, was the one being the jerk. During change of class she navigated the flow of bodies coursing through the main hall until she surfaced in the media center doorway. She had to think.

Mr. Malory could explain the scoring.

Her breathing grew faster at the idea of a private interview. What if he thought she just wanted to be alone with him?

"Oh, for Pete's sake. He's above that," she said out loud.

"Above what?" The hand that clapped her shoulder sparkled with multiple rings setting off shiny pink nails.

Bernadette turned, already smiling. If they had beauty pageants for plump people, Lucy Kestenberg could be Miss Michigan. Even Wickham's cheerleaders, no slouches at cosmetic enhancement, admired the way Ms. K.'s flawless grooming and vividly colored, ultra-stylish suits made a size l6 seem like something to shoot for.

Ms. Kestenberg was Wickham's librarian. Besides stocking required books, she always kept Sarah Sloan mysteries on her "Too Good to Miss" shelf. Sarah Sloan's heroines were usually librarians, or else the crime was committed in a library, or maybe the murderer had endowed the library. It was an enormous source of satisfaction to both Ms. Kestenberg and Bernadette that someone had finally realized how exciting a library could be. They had a running bet to see who could read the latest one first. Ms. K. had won on *Death Overdue*, but Bernadette had triumphed by ordering *Subscription Expired* over the Internet.

This year Ms. K. had taken over as coach of the debate team. She was coming along nicely, in spite of a tendency to harp too much on sportsmanship. "You must *persuade*. Arrogance is not persuasive," she'd say.

Each time she heard this, Bernadette would exclaim, "Tell me about it," and wish someone would give such counsel to Pinehurst, who needed it.

"I've been keeping an eye out for you," the librarian said now. Her fuchsia suit blazed against denim-clad students like a burning bush in the desert. Loud noises might be prohibited in the library, but Ms. Kestenberg's clothes were a visual yell. "Winning the Classics Contest! Your class must be wild. I hope this makes up for some of those debate losses."

Bernadette grinned. "It helps, I'll tell you that." She stepped into the library. The hall noise dropped to a distant roar among the tall shelves and carpeted floor. "In fact, I meant to ask you— didn't you help proctor that test?"

"I certainly did. The rules say you need three faculty members present. Mrs. Standish was there, too." Back at her desk Ms. K. eased into her swivel chair and started clicking away at her keyboard.

Bernadette moved closer. "Ms. K., we got a *ninety-two percent* on that test."

"Frank Malory told me. It's wonderful."

"Yeah. It would be, except—we couldn't have. None of us knew all those books." She thought of Lori. "Some of us couldn't spell them."

Ms. K. looked up. A flicker of unease showed deep in her mascara-fringed eyes. Just a micro-tightening of facial muscles that was hard to detect, but Bernadette could have sworn it was there. "Well, now, I wouldn't know about that. They graded the tests at NCS."

"Mr. Malory didn't grade them first?"

"Oh, no." Ms. Kestenberg patted her lacquered hair. "NCS is as security-mad as the CIA, to hear Frank. He knows all about it. They grade the answer sheets by hand and then again by machine. Just in case."

"In case of — ?"

"Mistakes, of course." Her look dared Bernadette to suggest something else. "Anyone can make mistakes."

"Ms. K., I can't help thinking there's *been* a mistake." Bernadette glanced around the library, but no one was paying attention. "Maybe our answer sheets got mixed up with St. John's Gifted, or Detroit Country Day. I'd know better if I could see the test."

Ms. K. hit the return key. "The instructions say distinctly that the test is not to be copied. They make you send it right back that day, along with the answer sheets."

"Oh." Bernadette wondered if she'd imagined that eye flash of alarm. "Well, I'll see you at the debate tournament Saturday," she said. The typing never slowed.

She had almost reached the door when Ms. Kestenberg called, "Bernadette."

"Yes?"

Ms. K. motioned her closer. "There *is* a copy of the test."

"But you said — "

"Mr. Malory has it. He left me in charge toward the end of the period while he used the copier in the teachers' lounge." On Ms. K.'s monitor, the HELP screen flashed over and over. "Frank — Mr. Malory — wanted a copy to prepare your class for the AP exam. Teachers are always using old state tests to get kids ready for the MEAPs. I didn't see any harm."

MEAPs were Michigan tests for checking that students learned at least some basic skills. "Me neither," Bernadette said.

It was as though she'd given the librarian absolution. Ms. K. exhaled noisily and smiled at her. "I bet every school who took it has a copy of the stupid thing if we only knew." She stabbed Cntrl/Break savagely. "Oh, hell's *bells*. Sorry, Bernadette. I wondered at the time whether I should have objected, but it was — awkward." She twisted one of her rings around her finger several times. "Without being a complete Goody Two-Shoes. Frank Malory is very persuasive. People don't realize."

Bernadette's face mirrored the arch of Ms. K.'s well-shaped eyebrows. There passed between them a woman-to-woman look exactly like one Bernadette might exchange with Nadine. "People realize, Ms. K. I think the hamsters in the science room realize."

That look again.

"The *girl* hamsters," she added, a beat ahead of the librarian. They laughed in rueful, unspoken acknowledgement of the power of sex.

Why isn't Ms. K. married? Bernadette wondered suddenly. Some man was missing out on a good thing.

Ms. K. was saying what did you want to bet that the whole thing was graded on a curve. This seemed to reassure her. "And now," she said, "I've got something for you. A little reward, you might say." She rooted around under her desk and produced a shopping bag.

"Murder by the Book!" Bernadette opened it with care. Hardback. Shiny dust jacket, not even entered into the computer yet. She sniffed the crisp pages. If they could turn this smell into perfume she'd bathe in it. "Thanks, Ms. K. I can't wait to read it."

She was late to study hall, but the teacher in charge didn't bother asking to see her pass. Students like Bernadette Terrell didn't cause trouble no matter where they'd been.

In her room after dinner Bernadette struggled against the lure of an unread Sarah Sloan. Stubbornly she finished her trigonometry, a French essay, and a synopsis of the first three cantos of Dante's *Inferno*. This she typed. She didn't have to, but appearances counted, as Martha always said. When it came to her English homework Bernadette allowed the possibility that her mother, in this rare instance, might be right.

It was after eleven before she crawled into bed clutching *Murder by the Book* like a dieter with a

pilfered éclair. She would never confess such common taste to Mr. Malory, but she found great comfort in mysteries, where you knew for sure who the villains were, and who were the heroes. None of that Fitzgerald ambiguity to make you unsure who to root for. With Sarah Sloan you knew where you were. Bernadette liked that in a book.

But tonight trusty Sarah let her down. To be fair, it wasn't the book's fault. The story began with a bang as always. The clever heroine—a grad student in library science—stayed one step ahead of her readers.

But Bernadette's mind kept returning to test scores. *Could* someone have smuggled a massive cheat sheet into the test? It would have had to be on a microchip to escape Mr. Malory. Nor would one cheat sheet have sufficed. *Five* of them were Wizards. That called for fraud on a grander scale.

Sherlock Holmes said that once you ruled out the impossible, the improbable was left. Which meant . . .

Mr. Malory? Bernadette lay in bed and laughed out loud. Ridiculous. Yes, he'd copied the test, but for a good reason. That was a far cry from altering their scores. If he'd wanted to cheat he'd have used proctors a lot dimmer than Ms. K. and eagle-eyed Spic 'n' Span.

Besides, he was death on cheating. A senior debater had told her of an incident from Honors

English the year before, Mr. Malory's first year at Wickham. He'd caught a boy copying from another student's paper. He'd torn the boy's test in half and called the parents in for a conference.

Bernadette had shivered at the tale. She would never cheat, naturally, but if she *had* cheated, and been caught, she'd have gone straight to the hardware store for rope to hang herself.

What about Ms. K.? She craved a laptop computer. And she had been alarmed about something today, Bernadette would swear to it.

She creased the bedsheet into a thick wad of pleats. To suspect Ms. Kestenberg of rigging a test was just as asinine as Nadine said. They *knew* Ms. K. She was too conscientious, too likable, too sporting. What was it she always said when she checked their evidence cards to make sure they said what was claimed for them? "Truth is the safest lie." That flash of conscience had been remorse over the copied test, no doubt. Or maybe she'd left the water running in the teachers' lounge. Ms. K. could have nothing to hide.

Bernadette went back to her book. The heroine was driving a car the wrong way down a one-way street while a former library volunteer shot at her from a helicopter.

What about Mrs. Standish?

Ah. Now *there* was a suspect. Telling them how proud the superintendent would be of them, as though she'd had anything to do with it! Perhaps she had. And the Lifetime Achievement Award as an incentive—something shifty there. *And* the tests had sat in the main office until Federal Express picked them up. Opportunities galore.

Bernadette nodded with decision and finished the chapter. Deep down she knew the odds that foul play really had occurred were as likely as her mother winning the Julia Child Cooking Award. But the sheer unlikeliness of the whole thing would not let her alone. She meant to investigate. The way she saw it, one of three things had happened:

1. The fates had conspired, and Wickham really *had* won;
2. Someone had cheated;
3. NCS had screwed up.

If it was (2) or (3), people were in for a very rude shock. If it was (1)—she was leaning toward Ms. K.'s curve theory—she and Nadine could set about humiliating Pinehurst with easy minds.

Bernadette fell asleep trying to decide what a Sarah Sloan detective would wear to question a key witness with very green eyes.

chapter six

> I am giddy, expectation whirls me round.
> The imaginary relish is so sweet
> That it enchants my sense.
> —Shakespeare, *Troilus and Cressida*

On Wednesday Bernadette missed her first book bee question of the year. And Mr. Malory wore a collarless shirt to school.

Lori Besh pretended to pant. "I saw chest hair!" she whispered to the girl beside her.

Who was Nadine. Who giggled.

Honestly. Mr. Malory's linen shirt was hardly in the thong category. Even by tilting her head to float her contacts into prime viewing position, Bernadette saw only a discreet expanse of smooth, male neck.

Which was quite enough.

"Now that you've finished *Gulliver's Travels*— you *have* finished it, haven't you?—name something the Yahoos do that the Houyhnhnms never do." He'd lined them up into book bee teams. Three a week, he'd ruled, until the Bowl.

Maybe it was the shirt. But when David muttered, "I forget," Bernadette's own mind went blank. The rest of her team—Nadine, Lori, and LaShonda—looked to her as usual.

Um, um . . . Houyhnhnms were horses. Yahoos were barbaric people. "They can . . . juggle?" For once her tentative act was real.

Mr. Malory drew a finger across his throat. Hoots of glee came from the Blues. Anthony Cirillo smirked and said, "Yahoos lie."

"Big deal. It's only one," LaShonda whispered to her.

Bernadette appreciated LaShonda's support. She just wished it had come from Nadine, who usually stood in that spot. Apparently the suggestion that Wickham might not be a winner still rankled. Showing up a "real" Korean like Glenn Kim must mean more to her partner than Bernadette had realized.

Students vanished at the bell like bungee jumpers on faulty cord. Bernadette dawdled at her desk. "Mr. Malory?"

He looked up. "Ms. Terrell. What can I do for you?"

"I wanted to ask you—about the Classics Contest?"

He raised his eyebrows attentively. Bernadette clutched her notes and approached his desk. Unconsciously she slipped into her best argument-summarizing manner as she outlined her concerns:

the unread books, her own estimated score, the possibility of an answer sheet mix-up. "I can't figure out how we could have *averaged* ninety-two percent," she finished in apology.

The tiny tic under Mr. Malory's eye jumped.

Panic hit her. *Oh dear God I'm right. Someone did cheat, and he's trying to figure out who.*

He reached out his hand for her paper. "May I?" He scanned the many calculated score combinations with which she had estimated her classmates' literary knowledge. His guarded expression gave way to a laugh.

"I see you've spent some time on this. Good heavens." He smiled, and her stomach went into its airborne routine. "The fact is, the scores were normalized."

"Ah." Bernadette nodded sagely. "Normalized."

"'Percentaged,' if you will. Based on the total results." He started pulling out drawers from his desk. "Each school received a raw score and a calculated one. I have the scoring formula here somewhere. You can read it for yourself." He flicked through hanging files. "Well, I can't put my hands on it at the moment, but I will get it to you."

"I *knew* we hadn't gotten all those questions right." Bernadette was delighted to be right and a winner, too. "Could you give me an example of how normalizing works?"

Mr. Malory leaned against the front of his desk. She caught a faint trace of almond-spice scent. It was "Intrigue," she knew, having sampled all the testers at Hudson's cologne counter. They should need a license to sell it.

"Certainly," he said. "First, the NCS people score the answer sheets. The highest student becomes one hundred percent. Then the top five individual scores from each school are calculated as a percentage of that single score."

Bizarre. "You mean, say I got an eighty-five percent on the test—"

"If that was the highest overall score, it would be calculated as one hundred percent." He paused. He took off his glasses, and his eyes looked more gray than green. "In actual fact, you got an eighty-seven percent. The highest score in the state."

"I *did*? Wow." Bernadette couldn't control her smile. She pulled her calculator from her back pocket and punched in some numbers. "So an eighty percent would be recorded as—eighty-seven into eighty—a ninety-two?"

"Precisely." He seemed pleased. "Wickham didn't actually average ninety-two on the test. Our raw scores were simply normalized to that."

The whole process seemed a roundabout way for a computer company to proceed, Bernadette said. Not that she wasn't tickled to death to have won—

"Let's consider it from their perspective." Mr. Malory leaned back as though there were nowhere he'd rather be. "NCS *wants* people to talk about how rugged their test is. You think those bogus scholars at Pinehurst weren't sweating it out? Do you think *any* school, no matter how much shrubbery it plants, could cover all that material?"

"It *is* a pretty school, isn't it," Bernadette said pensively. At debate tournaments Pinehurst hosted, she and Nadine had privately exclaimed at the putting-green luxury of the campus. Bleachers with awnings. Cobblestone walkways. Bathrooms with working tampon machines. "I wouldn't mind some of that fanciness at Wickham."

"No, *no*. That's the beauty of this win, Bernadette, don't you see?" He had that "Oh, you Americans" tone as he chopped the air with one hand. "It proves that you don't need minor Impressionists hanging in the hallways, so-called experts in Elizabethan drama, students dressed like an army of plums. What counts is how well a school fosters its students' natural competitiveness."

She loved how he said her name. "You think so?"

"Of course." He looked straight at her and inclined his head forward. Bernadette treasured his words in advance.

"I've known since September that this was Wickham's year." He wouldn't confide this to just anyone, she saw. "You and your friend Nadine have brains like sponges. It's inspiring. And Anthony Cirillo is nobody's fool, though he can show a maturity deficit at times. This team can have The Power, Bernadette. Just you wait."

She would wait. She would wait *forever.*

He broke the spell then by glancing up at the classroom clock. Bernadette scooped up her books. She wanted to race out and memorize Goethe in the original German. To sleep with Greek myths under her pillow. To write sonnets better than Keats. "Ode to a Gray Shirt" sprang to mind.

"You're a good teacher, Mr. Malory," she managed to say.

His smile would have melted her retainer, except that she'd removed it before class. "I have good students, that's the secret. Shall we adjourn to the cafeteria?"

Nadine would freak. "Sure," Bernadette said.

He didn't go so far as to eat *with* her, naturally. But he went through the line right behind her, which forced Bernadette to select her food with care.

Finally she ordered chicken rice soup and crackers. The fare of someone interestingly frail, not a teenager who ate like a healthy lion.

Mr. Malory walked off toward the teachers' lounge while Bernadette scanned the room. Lori Besh's eyes were popping, which made Bernadette grin. But where was Nadine? If she would only show herself, Bernadette would grovel on demand. Wait'll her partner heard that they could have The Power.

She gulped down her soup and got back in line for some real food. The stewed plums on ice made her think of Pinehurst's blazers. Mr. Malory certainly had their number. She thought of something. During his brief time in America, when had Mr. Malory visited That School?

chapter seven

. . . be wery careful o' widders all your life . . .
—Charles Dickens, *The Pickwick Papers*

In biology, the sight and smell of the formaldehyde-filled grass frog on the lab table caught Bernadette off-guard. She'd forgotten about today's dissection.

Breathing as lightly as she could, she cut into the little stomach just as an office runner came into the room. Bernadette Terrell was wanted at the principal's office. Bernadette was out the door before Mr. Fodor finished giving the message. Of course her parents *might* have been killed in a car crash. But it was much more likely that some administrative mania for detail had uncovered an outdated tetanus shot. And meanwhile, no frog guts.

Down at the office, Mrs. Standish had stepped out. It was she, apparently, who wanted to see Bernadette. While Bernadette waited, she looked on the bulletin board for the yellow NCS brochure, resolved to study the Scoring section this time instead of Prizes. But the brochure was gone.

"Classics Contest? Isn't it up on the board?" The secretary's attention was split between dispensing change for the telephone to one boy while keeping a close watch on a pasty-faced girl who stared down at her own shoes as though they were a crystal ball.

The girl hiccuped and swayed toward the wastebasket.

"*Oh*, no you don't, missy, you can just make it to the girls' room —"

Bernadette had seen enough stomach contents for one day. She backed out, turned, and ran smack into Mrs. Standish.

The principal steadied her with a surprisingly strong grip. Bernadette shifted into respectful principal-mode. "I'm awfully sorry, Mrs. Standish. Are you all right?"

From behind them came unmistakable sounds of gastric distress. "Fine, fine. Oh, dear. Let's just use the other door. . . ." Mrs. Standish steered Bernadette out the main door and around the corner, to where a hallway led past the guidance counselors' rooms and back to the principal's private domain. "Don't spare the Lysol, Katherine," she called into the reception area as she ushered Bernadette inside. She closed the door firmly behind them.

"Have a seat, dear. Just let me see . . ." Mrs. Standish settled herself behind her desk and picked up a manila folder on which Bernadette could read her own name. Maybe she had won another award.

While Mrs. Standish fussed with papers, Bernadette looked around. She'd never been back here before. On the desk was a framed photograph of—she craned forward—a kindly looking gray-haired man in a suit and tie. Mr. Spic 'n' Span, she presumed. On the wall to her right hung a framed blowup of a cartoon from Wickham's student paper, the *Warrior Cry*. Bernadette recognized David Minor's handiwork and smiled. The cartoon showed a castle wall with turrets and WICKHAM scrolled in an ornate arch. On the ramparts helmeted warriors (labeled HALL MONITORS) poured cauldrons of lye and boiling water down upon giant germs on horseback, who screamed "AAARGH!" in capital letters and waved swords in their tentacles. A crowned Queen of Clean beamed from a tower window. The caption read: "Soap and Water: Stop the Filth!" Bernadette was a little surprised to see it there. Spic 'n' Span must have a sense of humor after all.

"Is it Bernadine *Terr*·ell or Terr·*ell*?" Mrs. Standish asked.

"Terr·*ell*. Berna∂ette Terrell."

"Terr·ELL," Mrs. Standish murmured, making a note. "I don't get to know the students the way I did when I was teaching." She looked up. "I taught business typing for twenty years, did you know that? Of course," she added, as though anxious to establish her academic credentials, "I can teach English, too. I always pitched in on *Silas Marner* during flu season."

Bernadette smiled politely. If there weren't going to be refreshments she'd just as soon get to the point.

Mrs. Standish clasped her hands together on the desk. "Is there anything you want to tell me, dear?" she asked, with the resolutely unshockable air of some social workers and homicide detectives.

"Pardon?"

"Anything you want to confide in me? About the NCS Classics Contest, you know. Any concerns, any worries—about the scoring, for instance?" She began to doodle with her pen, at the same time shooting sharp little glances across the desk.

Ms. K.! It could only have been her. "Oh, that! At first I was a little surprised to hear we had such high scores. Not everyone in my class is . . . a big reader, I guess you could say. But then Mr. Malory explained it to me."

The pen stopped in mid-doodle. "Mr. Malory explained it?"

"Uh-huh. About how they normalize the scores." The principal looked at her in mystification. "You might call it, percentaging?"

"Percentaging. Oh, right. Good, good." Mrs. Standish scratched behind her ear with her pen. "How *do* they do it? I've always been unclear on that myself."

This surprised Bernadette, who had just assumed a principal would know these things, but she obligingly went through the arithmetic lesson she'd heard two hours ago. When she finished, Mrs. Standish was wearing a frown of concentration. "So that's how it's done! Thank you, dear. You have a gift for explaining things. And I'm glad you did, in case someone at the next school-board meeting asks about it." She pushed off with one hand, spun her chair completely around very fast, and came to rest in the exact position as a second before. Seriously, she asked, "So you're comfortable now with all aspects of this competition? No lingering suspicion that anyone might have, oh, made a mistake? Notified the wrong school? Cheated, anything like that?"

Bernadette was trying to convince herself she'd seen that chair spin thing. "No, no problems. I'm fine."

"Because I want every single Wizard ready to work. You wouldn't believe how people are reacting to this, Bernadette. The superintendent has called twice to make sure I'm taking this seriously. I told him he doesn't need to worry! And two parents who work for NCS called to say how pleased they are that their child's school has a team in the Bowl. They said it looks very good for them at work. And—I loved this—one of the admissions staff at Michigan State told us just this week that she'd never realized Wickham was a private school!" She chortled, and this time Bernadette's smile was genuine. *That* was funny. Mrs. Standish gave a sharp bark of laughter. "Ha! Private school!" She arranged her face more solemnly. "Now, then. What is it Coach Finley tells his players? 'Kick butt'? How about if you and your teammates go in front of those TV cameras and kick Pinehurst's butt!" Another chortle escaped her, and again she spun her chair around. "Or butts, I should say. Private school! What do you think about *that*?"

Bernadette thought Wickham had a principal with a few screws loose. "That's a good one, all right. I'd better get back to class now, Mrs. Standish." There was something odd about this whole interview. Bernadette welcomed the chance to ponder it over a dead frog.

On the way out to the bus, she heard girls' voices floating from the gym.

"Come on, Warriors, go! Go! Left, right, ready, GO!"

Bernadette peeked in the open doors. The varsity pompon squad—as opposed to the j. v., she loved that they had a farm team for pompon—posed in a pyramid in front of the empty bleachers, big green W's blazing from their chests. Lori Besh stood like smiling steel on the bottom row while two squad-mates ground their sneakers into her shoulders.

Bernadette imagined that weight pressing into her own neck, and tensed. She exhaled very slowly. The group went through some routines, moving with a polish and precision that even Bernadette recognized as top-notch. She could not mock their work ethic. She thought of the Governor's All-Star Pompon Competition that Lori had dumped like it had fleas, and said a word even easy-going Joe Terrell would have washed her mouth out for.

This Bowl thing was getting complicated.

chapter eight

> Do I contradict myself?
> Very well then I contradict myself,
> (I am large, I contain multitudes.)
> — Walt Whitman, *Song of Myself*

"'Kick butts.' Can you imagine? I don't believe she ever taught English. Unless it was English slang for immigrants." Bernadette blew into her Styrofoam cup. The coffee was too hot to sip even if she'd wanted to, which she didn't, especially. Coffee repelled her. But it was so adult. Nadine was the one who'd been hungry. Bernadette was so relieved that Nadine was speaking to her again—her partner's triumph at cutting biology without getting caught had made her forget she was mad at Bernadette—that when Nadine intercepted her at the bus line and suggested they stop at McDonald's, Bernadette had agreed readily.

Across the booth from her, Nadine wielded a plastic knife with the skill of a surgeon as she removed batter-fried coating from her fish fillet. "Maybe instead of *Washington Square*, she taught *Washington Butt*."

"Yeah. Or *David Copperbutt*."

"Tess of the D'Urberbutts."

"Moby Butt." Bernadette considered that. It was actually an improvement.

"I hate to break this to you, but lots of people say 'butt.'"

"Oh, I know that. But it's crude. And from a principal!" Bernadette shuddered, and gingerly tested her coffee with her fingertip. She poured in another creamer. "Though she wasn't as bad as people say—she didn't make me take my shoes off at the door like I thought. But don't you think it's strange she'd call me down to her office just to make sure I was 'comfortable'? It was like she was afraid I *did* see something suspicious. Like it was her duty to check it out, but she hoped to God there was nothing to it."

Nadine saw nothing strange about it. "It shows she's paying attention."

"Oh, she's paying attention. You should have heard her crowing over someone thinking we were a private school. I think it made her year. Us winning the Bowl might just unhinge her altogether." Bernadette pictured Spic 'n' Span spiraling into the sky in her swivel chair.

"She has a lot riding on this," Nadine said. "My dad told us she's still paying off medical bills from when her husband died. He had a brain tumor. They tried all kinds of cures—I think they even went to Mexico—but the insurance didn't pay for everything."

Bernadette paused in midchew. "I didn't know that." A vision forced itself into her mind of Spic 'n' Span sitting in an antiseptic kitchen late at night, calculating how long she had to live. What a year, a month, would cost. A mangy dog at her feet, a cup of cold tea at her elbow. A man's old suits and wide neckties all tagged for a garage sale. . . . She sipped her coffee and grimaced. Her next sentence surprised even herself. "I don't suppose it's possible *she* cheated?"

Nadine regarded her with pity. "Bet, give it up. How's she supposed to have cheated?"

"Don't laugh. But the tests went to the office to be picked up by Federal Express. They would have been there long enough for her to change our answers." The more Bernadette thought about it, the more sense this theory made. It would certainly explain how Lori and David had achieved that out-of-character spurt of brilliance. "It's like that picture puzzle of the old woman and the vase. You look at it one way, and Spic 'n' Span is just doing her job; close the other eye, and she's trying to find out if I'll blow the whistle on a fraud she cooked up to weasel money out of the school board. It's like Sarah Sloan always says—half the time you don't know who the bad guys are until they tip their hand."

"Sorry," Nadine said, not sounding sorry. "But I can only see it the first way, no matter how many eyes I close. Hey, not to change the subject, but do you see that guy behind the counter? Don't turn around! With the really cute—"

"You know what?" Bernadette slapped the tabletop. "I must be crazy. Spic 'n' Span is so weird, it's a wonder she remembers where her office is. She *couldn't* have changed our tests in cold-blood. You're right. Forget I mentioned it. The important thing now is to clobber Pinehurst."

Nadine pulled her gaze away from the cashiers behind the counter. "You mean you're prepared to kick butt?"

Bernadette flinched. Then saw that Nadine was laughing. "You could say that." She reached for a french fry and knocked over her nearly full cup of coffee. The milky liquid raced toward Nadine.

"Eee-you!" Nadine scrambled out of the booth.

"Sorry, sorry, oh, dammit . . ." Bernadette grabbed the lone napkin and tried to mop up the puddle, but it was like using a Q-tip to soak up a river.

A McDonald's worker materialized from nowhere.

"Thanks." She accepted his fistful of napkins and waited for him to leave.

He didn't. "Hey. My brother's in your English

class," he announced, as though delivering good news. "You know, Anthony?" When he smiled his teeth flashed white against a fresh olive complexion. He could have stepped out of a TV commercial. Bernadette read his name tag: ASST. MGR. VINCE CIRILLO.

She gaped at Nadine, who was not looking at her. McAss had a brother?

Asst. Mgr. Vince took the soggy napkins and stuffed them in the trash can, talking the whole time. "Man, Anthony's all hyped about that book thing with Pinehurst. I hope your team smashes them. If you're in the market, I know a guy giving three to two."

Bernadette's forehead creased.

"On Wickham," he added helpfully.

Nadine came out of her trance. "You mean, like, a bookie?"

Her rough voice seemed to fascinate him. "You got it. But the minimum bet's twenty." He shouted over the counter for a fresh coffee, then looked at their baffled faces. "Dollars, that is. In case you're thinking pesos."

Oh, joy. Another Cirillo smart aleck. He did look like Anthony, in a way, tall and athletic, with the black curly hair Nadine had already noticed. But Vince was clearly older, with an air of worldliness Anthony lacked. He had a crooked wise-guy smile *some* people might find attractive.

"Thanks." Nadine purred. "We'll think about it."

Bernadette found her voice. "Hey, Vince?"

"Yo."

"How'd you know who we were?"

"Anthony said. He just came on drive-thru." Vince motioned toward the counter. Sure enough, there was Anthony's curly head with an earphone stuck in one ear. He looked up from the soda machine and waved.

Vince eyed Nadine. "You girls mind if I sit with you a minute?"

"Actually, we're in the middle of—"

"Sit here." Nadine patted the bench beside her.

Vince gave her a smile that probably sold a lot of meal combos and went to fetch Bernadette a new coffee.

"What are you doing?" Bernadette kept her voice low with an effort. "He's a *Cirillo*."

"He's cute," Nadine said, and then it was too late. Vince came back with two coffees, one for himself. He dropped a pile of creamers on the table. Bernadette dumped all of them into her cup, with four sugars.

"You know what? We just hired a Chinese kid. I bet you could talk to him better than me," Vince said.

Bernadette stirred busily so Nadine would not see the grin spreading across her face. He might as well have offered them chopsticks.

Nadine's smile vanished. "I am not Chinese," she said icily. "I was born in Korea." She did not call him a cretin, but it was in her voice.

He heard it. "Korea, huh? That's cool. I'm terrible at telling what people are just by looking at them, unless they're black, and then they could be Jamaican or Puerto Rican or . . ." He trailed off. Or Cuban or Kenyan or really tanned—Bernadette almost felt sorry for him. "I guess Korean's a lot different from Chinese, am I right?"

"Right," Nadine said shortly. She paused. A smidgen less coldly, she said, "Well, I think it is. I don't happen to speak either one."

Vince's nose twitched like a beagle's at her defensive tone. He leaned toward her. "I'll let you in on a little secret." He tapped his chest with one finger. "Me neither."

Nadine choked on her drink, and even Bernadette's lips twisted. Vince *was* kind of funny.

Nadine thought so. Bernadette slunk down in her seat as her fellow National Honor Society officer tittered like a bad actress in a Tennessee Williams play, tossed her ruler-straight hair, and took off her glasses every few minutes to gaze into Vince's eyes.

Vince lapped it up.

Bernadette finished her chicken sandwich. And the remaining fries. And the scraped-off fish-coating on Nadine's tray. She was seriously considering the beige sludge in her cup when Vince finally said something of interest.

He wanted to know what kinds of questions they'd get in the Classics Bowl.

"Oh, stuff like who wrote *Tristram Shandy*. What was the setting for Thoreau's most famous book, how many syllables in an iamb. That kind of thing." Nadine started to flick back her hair, caught Bernadette watching her, and dropped her hand into her lap. "Like *Jeopardy!* Only all the categories will be literature. You know—books."

Vince nodded. "I love that show." He spoke with heartfelt sincerity. "You get guys on there who don't know sh—much, and they'll bet the farm on Final Jeopardy and get lucky." He shook his head over gut-clenching finales of the past. "No offense, but it's always your men players who take the biggest risks." He tore his eyes away from Nadine. "So, Bernadette. My little brother says if you get run over by a truck, the Wizards are dead meat. I guess you know your Shakespeare, huh?"

Bernadette was flattered in spite of herself. Anthony might toss margarine pats up on the cafeteria ceiling so they'd melt and fall down on people's heads, but he knew smart. She shrugged. "I know some."

Vince waited. Nadine nodded encouragement.

Honestly. "'. . . foul deeds will rise, / Though all the earth o'erwhelm them, to men's eyes.'"

"Cool," Vince said. "What is it?"

"Hamlet."

"Bet's got a photographic memory," Nadine boasted.

"Yeah, that's what Anthony said. But can she remember enough to beat Pinehurst's butt one more time?"

From Vince you expected "butt." That wasn't what made Bernadette quiver as though an invisible spitball had glanced off her neck. As though his words had triggered them, other voices set up a clamor in her head.

"She'll look fine at the Classics Bowl, giving 'em hell."

"Glenn Kim. Uriah Heep. What I wouldn't give to humiliate him."

"I've never won anything for brains."

"This team can have The Power, Bernadette."

"The superintendent called twice. A private school—ha!"

A plastic knife jabbed her arm. Nadine was glaring at her.

"Sorry. What'd you say?"

"Vince wants to know if you think we have a chance—"

"Of a snowball in hell," Vince put in.

"Of winning. I said we were just talking about that." Nadine put her glasses back on and stared meaningfully through them. "Weren't we?"

Bernadette hiccuped. She had no proof the scores had been fixed. And no intention, now, of looking for any.

The Power surged through her veins. "Vince?" she said. "Do you own any cropland? Wheat futures, soybeans? 'Cause we can help you triple your investment."

Nadine gurgled. She turned to Vince, and her black eyes glistened. "My partner is saying you should bet the farm—on the Wizards."

Nadine drove the long way home without being reminded.

The day was cool but sunny. Mr. Malory was out in the parking lot of his apartment complex, waxing the Porsche.

They drove by, and Bernadette hid her face in the shoulder harness. They'd passed Kmart before her insides returned to normal. "Did he see us?" she demanded.

"I don't think so."

He'd had on an old T-shirt. It was surprising what you could notice in two seconds. His bare arms had rubbed the gleaming hood over and over, his muscles visible (to the keen eye) from the highway.

Oh, that she might be a fender on that car.

chapter nine

Our interest's on the dangerous edge of things.
　　　　　　　　　　　　—Robert Browning

Mr. Malory scheduled their first strategy session for Thursday night.

Not so fast, was the reaction he got. Sure, they wanted to win, but Thursday was a bad night. Lori had dance class, Anthony had to work, Nadine had some commitment she didn't identify, Bernadette had to meet some freshmen debaters at the Creighton library. David had nothing to do but joined in the protest companionably.

Mr. Malory watched them with lifted eyebrows. One by one the objections petered out. By Wednesday everyone had rearranged their schedules. The Classics Bowl was an American institution their teacher took very seriously.

Bernadette turned the key in the ignition. Nothing.

"Oh, no." This was the Suburban's revenge on her for all the mean things she had said about it. "You're a good little truck," she crooned. "You're not old and smelly at *all.* I'm proud to be seen in you."

She turned the key again. From deep in the bowels of the engine came a tiny protesting whine, followed by a silence of pure malice.

"Be that way, you sorry piece of junk."

She stared at the dashboard clock. Her parents were at a church meeting. She'd have to call someone on the team.

In the kitchen she grabbed the phone and cursed Mr. Malory for holding this first meeting in Ann Arbor. It was forty-five minutes away, for Pete's sake. But he'd reserved a private conference room at the university library, with multiple copies of the books they'd need, plus temporary borrowing privileges. Courtesy of the Classics Contest research committee, whose chairwoman taught at U of M. The perfect setup, he called it.

Would Pinehurst be there, Nadine had wanted to know. Her new Korean-English dictionary had taught her how to say "your fly is open," and she wanted to spring it on Glenn Kim.

Mr. Malory seemed glad someone had asked. No, Pinehurst had declined. Their coach had been offended at the suggestion that a university library might be superior to the Pinehurst collection. The ironic look that accompanied this sent a unifying ripple of disdain through the Wizards.

But now, frantically dialing Nadine, Bernadette

didn't think Pinehurst so dumb. If the meeting had been at her own school she could have jogged there.

Nadine had left an hour ago, Mrs. Walczak said, sounding surprised. "She said she had to stop at McDonald's. I thought she was meeting you there, Bernadette."

"Nope, not tonight." Bernadette felt a flicker of annoyance. Nadine might at least have mentioned it.

She leafed through the school directory.

David, too, had already left. To pick up Anthony.

At the Besh's she got Lori's voice on the answering machine.

Her blood pressure rose. She would rather take an extra semester of gym than miss this meeting.

She dialed a number she knew by heart, though she'd never called it. It answered on the second ring. "You're there!" she said in a squeak.

"I live here, Bernadette."

He knew her voice! "I meant, I thought you'd have left by now. The thing is, my car won't start. I can't make it."

"I'm just out the door," Mr. Malory said crisply. "Where do you live?"

Bernadette gulped and told him. She grinned fiendishly at the refrigerator. Wait till Nadine heard.

The carpeting in the little car had been freshly shampooed. Brown leather seats gleamed with recent buffing. Bernadette sniffed appreciatively. Mr. Malory's car smelled as good as he did.

She could have stretched out her left arm and touched the driver's side window. The thought of what else she might touch made her dizzy.

"What kind of car is this?" She practically had to yell over the engine roar. She saw Mr. Malory's disbelieving glance. In Michigan, kindergartners knew Chryslers from Fords.

"I know it's a Porsche," she said quickly. "I meant what kind of Porsche."

"Oh," he said. "A '75 911 Carerra. My first major purchase in America, I'll have you know." He patted the leather-wrapped steering wheel affectionately. "What do you think of her?"

"She's fast."

He laughed, but they didn't slow down.

He wore jeans tonight, and a plain black shirt that turned his skin paler and made his eyes greener. No seat belt. Probably considered them sissy. But they were going at least eighty-five in a sixty-five zone, and that was zippy even for Detroit. Exciting, yes. Nonetheless, Bernadette tightened her shoulder strap and offered a quick prayer to St. Christopher.

Mr. Malory took a roll of peppermint Life Savers out of his shirt pocket. "Mint?"

"Thanks." Her fingers brushed his. "My dad had a Corvette once," she said, to make conversation.

He made a "pah" noise with his mouth, like a seat cushion being jumped on. "'Vettes," he said with scorn, and popped a Life Saver into his mouth. He cracked his window, rolled the excess foil between his fingers, and let the airstream suck it away.

She opened her mouth, then shut it. Her foot knocked against a case on the floor. "You sure have a lot of CDs."

"Here, let me get those out of your way." He kept one hand on the wheel and reached down for the CD case. The back of his hand grazed her leg. A sensation of such intense desire shot through her that she whimpered. She made herself cough. "Went down the wrong pipe." She gasped, and pounded her chest.

"False Idols." Mr. Malory fed a CD into the slot in the dashboard and gave no sign of noticing her distress. "You like them?"

"They're great," she croaked. She would have approved Gregorian chant. The driving pulse of electric guitars revved up her own heartbeat. Her leg tingled where he'd brushed it, as though his touch had scorched the denim.

He hummed to the music. "So, Bernadette. What do your parents think of our chances in the Classics Bowl?" She was "Ms. Terrell" in class, but "Bernadette" in his car. He flicked on the headlights, and two bright circles stabbed the dusk in front of them.

"My mother wants us to crush Pinehurst in front of the world. Although if one of the boys on their team asked me out afterward, that would be okay with her, too."

He laughed delightedly. "Beat 'em then join 'em, eh? I like your mother's attitude. What about your father?"

"Oh, whatever we do will be just fine with him. He's the one I'd like to win for, really."

Mr. Malory drummed his fingers on the wheel in time to the music. "Don't worry. At the risk of pleasing your mother, I'll bet you all a team dinner we win."

Bernadette was not short on confidence, but she could not feel as certain of victory as her teacher did.

Idly her fingers explored the compartment in the passenger door beside her. Nothing there except . . . matches? Yes, a book of matches. *His* matches. She slipped them into her jacket pocket. "Mr. Malory?"

"Hmm?"

"Do you think Mrs. Standish is . . . all there?"

"All where?"

"I mean, normal." One of her mother's phrases came to her. "Firmly anchored in reality."

His mouth quirked in amusement. "As much as any of us, I'd say. Why do you ask?"

Bernadette told him about the interview in the

principal's office. "So I told her what you'd told *me* about the percentaging."

"Did you, now?" Something in his voice made her glance at him. "And did that reassure her?"

"Oh, yeah. When I left she was practically dancing."

"Well, there you are, then. Nothing to worry about. I gather Peg is quite excited about the community support she's receiving. You Wizards have put Wickham on the map, metaphorically speaking. Naturally she'd want to investigate any rumors about her team's validity. But it sounds as though you set her mind at rest nicely." He seemed relieved himself, and his manner became more expansive. "To tell you the truth, Bernadette, even if there'd been a foul-up somewhere—which there wasn't, luckily—there's no doubt in my mind that this team could still outshine Pinehurst, given the chance. It's a question of motivation."

"Really?" That hard work could catch up with years of every cultural advantage was something she liked to say herself, all the time. But in her heart she was less sure. Hearing Frank Malory say it—and he should know, as educated as he was—worked on Bernadette like a drug. "Hey, did you know Lori invented a cheer for us? 'Break their pencils, stomp the finks, bust their buzzers, Pinehurst stinks!'"

She loved that she had made him laugh.

"Our Lori scored 720 on the verbal SAT. You didn't know? She'll do very well in the Bowl. And I never underestimate the power of red hair on elderly contest judges."

He gave her a subtle wink. It so clearly signaled their shared understanding about Lori's useful—but secondary—physical assets that Bernadette smiled, and didn't wonder until much later how sex appeal could possibly matter in a contest where you either knew the right answer or you didn't. Did he say 720?

He downshifted for the exit to Ann Arbor.

There were no empty meters near the library. Mr. Malory swung into a parking garage and stopped on a tiny space crisscrossed with diagonal blue lines.

"Uh—this is handicapped," Bernadette said.

The engine roar died away among the concrete pillars. "Not officially."

She had to climb over the gearshift to get out. They were in a loading zone against the wall meant for wide-opening doors or wheelchair lifts. Another vehicle—a Yugo, maybe, or a Schwinn— could still squeeze in beside them. And the remaining handicapped spots *were* empty.

Mr. Malory hoisted a fat briefcase out of the trunk. The boot, he called it. "All set?" he asked. "We're late." She had to run to keep up with him.

They climbed the broad stone stairs of the

library past a gauntlet of feminine appraisal that didn't seem to faze Bernadette's companion one whit. She sneaked a glance at their reflections in the entrance door. She looked older than sixteen, she decided. People might think they were a couple.

chapter ten

Theirs not to make reply,
Theirs not to reason why,
Theirs but to do and die.
—Alfred Lord Tennyson,
"The Charge of the Light Brigade"

The Wizards were watching cartoons.

Anthony had powered up a TV-VCR on its portable cart and when Bernadette and Mr. Malory arrived in the library conference room, he and David were reclining in their chairs with their feet propped up on the long table. More wheeled carts sagged under books that, even from the doorway, had a "required" smell about them. Lori was twisting Nadine's slippery hair into a French braid.

Both girls looked up at them with curiosity.

"My car wouldn't start," Bernadette said. She sat down, and Lori whispered, "Ooh. How'd you think of that?"

Bernadette had to laugh. She could see where, under certain circumstances, for short periods of time, Lori Besh might be fun.

Mr. Malory was all business tonight. He unpacked his briefcase and fed a tape into the VCR. On the TV, Roadrunner was replaced by fuzz. He produced a giant bag of chocolate chip cookies, asked if anyone needed to use the loo, then doused the lights.

Swelling orchestra music. NATIONAL COMPUTER SYSTEMS PRESENTS CLASSICS BOWL IX, announced big yellow letters.

"Hey, like the Super Bowl," David said.

"Shhh. I want to hear this." Bernadette blinked her lenses into focus and rested her elbows on the table.

Mrs. Phoebe Hamilton acted as moderator. They would hear three rounds of questions plus a Champion Round, she informed the studio audience in a plummy voice reminiscent of Queen Elizabeth. Thirty questions per round selected from twenty-five possible categories.

Teams could substitute players once a round, if they wished. Each team had one time-out per round. Only four of a team's five members played at a time.

The camera panned the teams. Pinehurst, of course. Versus St. John's School for the Gifted.

Pinehurst selected "Greeks."

"In Sophocles' tragedy *Oedipus the King*," Mrs. Hamilton read, "what is the answer to the Riddle of the Sphinx?"

It was an Open, meaning either team could answer. St. John's buzzed in first. "What is 'Man'?" a plump boy with glasses asked.

There was a ripple of laughter from the audience. "Man it is," Mrs. Hamilton said dryly. "No need to answer with a question. You're not on *Jeopardy!*"

The scorekeeper flipped over a card. Twenty points for St. John's.

Pinehurst exchanged slit-eyed glances. They all wore their school's purple blazer and tie, even the lone girl sitting out. Bernadette munched her cookie with a curled lip. Sexist pigs. At least St. John's had three girls on their team, although people who called themselves "gifted" gave her a pain.

The tape ran on. Wizard wisecracks came slower and soon stopped altogether as they were drawn into the drama on-screen. Bernadette already knew Pinehurst would win, but for most of the hour St. John's led. These scoring rules were courtesy of Mrs. Hamilton by way of the Mad Hatter. She jotted down notes in the dark, and felt Lori beside her doing the same.

A team could earn twenty points by answering an Open question, ten points for a Bonus. The scorekeeper kept a running tally.

"Name the next line in this well-known poem: 'The world is too much with us; late and soon . . .'"

Bzzz. A Pinehurst boy answered, "'Getting and spending, we lay waste our powers.'"

"Correct."

In the dark little room, Bernadette smelled fear. During the Champion Round, Pinehurst blew their gifted opponents away. It was just like *Double Jeopardy!*, Bernadette realized. The Champion Round could decide the match.

The last image on the screen before Mr. Malory snapped on the lights was St. John's looking like they'd all been run over by the same train.

The Wizards blinked. The cookies were nothing but crumbs, and so was their confidence.

"That was *fast*," Nadine said. "Wasn't that fast?"

"Aah, they missed a bunch," Anthony said.

"*They* did." Mr. Malory observed their stunned faces. "*You* won't."

"Mr. Malory, nobody could know all those books." Lori's voice had gone high and little. Sounded like the governor's pompon thing was looking more appealing.

"*Au contraire*, Ms. Besh. St. John's could have known much more. They simply didn't prepare." Like Merlin instructing young Arthur, their teacher brandished a rolled-up set of charts that he pinned one by one to the cork strip above the chalkboard. "I don't believe in 'gifted' students. I believe in students who work."

Now how did he know there'd be a place to hang those? Bernadette wondered. Behind Lori's back she poked Nadine. Debaters respected advance planning.

"Thirty-one categories." Mr. Malory tapped the first chart. Each box held a word or phrase.

"Every Bowl question has come from one of these categories."

"How do you know?" David asked.

"I counted. While you've been perfecting the art of portraiture, Mr. Minor, I've been studying twelve hours of Classics Bowl tape."

The others snickered. David put a hand over the sketch of his latest superheroine, who bore a suspicious resemblance to Lori Besh—if Lori owned thigh-high boots and a laser gun.

"How do you know they won't add new categories this year?" Nadine wanted to know.

"I don't. But if you learn these inside and out, you can cope with anything they add."

The next chart said: 1,000 QUESTIONS, 92 WRITERS, 297 WORKS. Then a table: NOVELS, 109; PLAYS, 31; LONG POEMS, 18; SHORT POEMS, 72; ESSAYS, 10; STORIES/FABLES, 33; SPEECHES, 7; BIBLE BOOKS, 17.

"Study this," he said.

Bernadette studied her teammates instead. They had a horrified roundness to their eyes, as though Jekyll had turned into Hyde in front of them.

More charts went up. One listed the names of books and—she squinted—authors. Very *small* names, typed and pasted on the chart. Hundreds of them.

"Two hundred ninety-seven works," Mr. Malory told the quiet room.

"Oh, good. I hate when it's more than three

hundred." But even Anthony sounded shaken.

"You've sure gone to a lot of trouble," Bernadette said.

Mr. Malory's smile flashed. "I feel responsible," he said. "I owe this team everything I can do to help you to a respectable showing. Though I must say, routing Pinehurst would be even better."

The fourth chart was their names.

They absorbed their individual categories. Each of them was Primary in some, Backup in others. Lori Besh had drawn a lot of the shorter poetry as well as Children's Classics. Mr. Malory lifted out a fat red binder, opened it, and handed around sets of stapled papers. Bernadette could have sworn hers was the thickest.

Mr. Malory said, "You see, Ms. Besh? With the proper organization, it *is* possible for one team to know it all. The right team."

The silence was as loaded as a grenade.

Anthony pulled the pin. "Wait a minute." His face was flushed, as though he'd leaned too close to the grill at work. He rolled his assignment sheets into a tube and used it to emphasize his words. "Let's just think about this. The Classics Bowl is in three weeks, right? *Some* of us have to eat and sleep and, just maybe, do *other* homework. We can't do this. It's impossible."

Bernadette's eyes swiveled back to Mr. Malory. Part of her agreed with Anthony. Covering the material just outlined would stretch speed-reading grad students in solitary confinement. For five bright but not brilliant high schoolers, it was madness.

And yet—another part of her wanted to cheer. Frank Malory *believed* in them. Couldn't Anthony feel it? Didn't he want to show the world they could do this thing?

Mr. Malory's left eyebrow rose one millimeter. "Do you want to win?"

"That's not fair," David grumbled. "We're talking ten grand. Sure we want to win."

"*I* want to win." Bernadette kicked Anthony's chair. "This is our year, Mr. Malory. You said so."

"My grandmother's lighting candles at church," Nadine said. "The last time she did that, we got a Polish pope. So yeah, *I* want us to win."

"I didn't drop out of the Governor's All-Star Pompon Competition to *lose*." Lori's blue eyes held a manic glitter, and the perfect chin was rock-like. She looked a lot smarter when she was angry, Bernadette decided.

Anthony shrank into his sweatshirt. "Don't look at me. I want to kick their butts. Did you see those wimpy outfits?"

Mr. Malory nodded. "Then you'll work. The Bowl is, as Mr. Cirillo has pointed out, only three and a half weeks from now. Obviously we won't discuss the books. You'll simply plow through them. Not the best way to meet them, I know, and for that I apologize. But next year, and—well, for the rest of your lives, actually—you can read them with the deliberation they deserve."

He gave them the smile that turned Bernadette's bones to Cream of Wheat. "You *can* do it. You can earn The Power." His voice held them mesmerized. "I wouldn't go forward with this if I didn't honestly believe you have it in you." *Especially you,* his green eyes said to Bernadette. *I'm counting on you.*

He was the Pied Piper.

Nadine wore a small, grim smile that dared Glenn Kim to get in her way. David's spine stiffened like a marine's. Lori's eyes went all starry like a musical heroine who's been kissed by the man of her dreams.

Anthony studied his kneecaps and didn't look like anything much. So that was normal.

chapter eleven

If there is a paradise on the face of the earth,
It is this, oh! it is this, oh! it is this.
— Mogul inscription in the Red Fort at Delhi

Nadine offered to drive Bernadette home, and Mr. Malory agreed, which Bernadette accepted with resignation. She couldn't expect two such rides in one lifetime.

Outside the library he thanked them for coming. Again he predicted a Wickham victory in the Classics Bowl. Then he set off down the street, away from the parking garage, whistling and tossing his keys.

Lori watched him with worried eyes. She said, to no one in particular, "Guys? I don't know about this."

"I do. He's crazy. Cracked, nutso." Anthony's hair lay oddly flat against his head, as if the curl had been scared out of it.

"I know what *I'm* going to do." David zipped and unzipped the breast pocket in his black leather jacket. He was fair and handsome and favored aggressively masculine attire, like camouflage shirts and work boots. He was also three inches shorter than Bernadette. Tonight he looked like a Boy Scout kidnapped by Hell's Angels. "I'm outta here. LaShonda was bummed not to make the team, and I'm about to do a noble thing."

Bernadette wanted to shake all of them. "You chickenshit, David Minor, you—"

"He's not chickenshit!" Anthony yelled. "He's just not hot for Malory! If you didn't get that simpy look every time Malory scratches himself you'd know he's completely—"

"Crazy?" Nadine cut in. "He's not crazy. Bet can read her whole list in a week and yours, too."

Bernadette shifted her backpack to her other shoulder. Let's not go overboard here, partner.

Nadine whirled on David. "Why didn't you tell Malory you're just not up to it? Hmmm? No guts?"

"He's not a whiner," Anthony snarled, and then Bernadette lost track of who said what.

"What do you call *this*—"

"I thought you guys would know all those books—"

"I hope Pinehurst wipes up the floor—"

"You're such a little quitter, that's—"

The shrill whistle shocked them into silence.

"Move along, people. You're blocking the sidewalk." The policewoman sounded bored. But her shiny gun in its leather holster was far from dull.

They moved. Under the streetlight at the corner, they stopped. They stood at an intersection on the

University of Michigan campus in downtown Ann Arbor. Restaurants, bars, and bookstores lined the streets in three directions, all open and bustling at nine-thirty at night. Aromas of curry and spare ribs and fresh-ground coffee drifted over sidewalk bins of sale books—thousands of them. Bernadette didn't know where to look first. An old man with a curling white mustache and a straw boater strummed a banjo while people paused to listen in the mild evening. Down the street a young girl played Gershwin on a saxophone, and people tossed money in her cap on the ground.

It was as far from familiar Creighton as Nepal. Bernadette's heart filled with a desperate longing to be a part of it. "I'm starved," she said, but she meant more than she could put into words. Starved for drama. For acceptance. For life after her mother's house.

And for food.

"Me, too." Anthony spoke mildly. "Chickenshit" might be a word he'd never heard.

"I'll go somewhere if someone has money," David offered generously.

Lori and Nadine admitted to being in funds. Hunger, it seemed, was one topic they could agree on.

They walked up one side of the block and down the other. They argued the merits of cafés versus cantinas, pizzerias, delis, bistros, and rathskellers, but in the end, Dmitri's Coney Island won out. It was cheap.

The waiter pushed two tables together.

In one booth a pair of young men clasped hands across the table. David nudged Anthony. Two tables away and paying them absolutely no attention, a group of girls in holey jeans pored over fat textbooks. Bernadette heard an Indiana drawl and a Brooklyn accent.

Four young men wearing turbans, Red Wings shirts, and pen protectors devoured chili dogs and shouted at each other in an Indian dialect. Probably arguing linear versus digital integrated circuits. Or hockey.

Bernadette breathed deeply in pure happiness. So this was college! Everyone looked so intent. So intellectual. Not a fake nail in the place—except Lori's.

"Bet, order." Nadine poked her. The waiter tapped his pad on the table.

"Oh. Um, a foot-long and a Coke, please."

Lori and David asked for coffee, to Bernadette's secret admiration, though when it came, Lori added milk and Sweet 'n' Low. David, ever the man's man, drank his black.

"That'll stunt your growth," Anthony said. "Oops, too late."

David burped in Anthony's ear.

"Cut it out!" Bernadette snapped. "You want people to think we're in high school?"

Nadine's throaty laugh drew smiles from the

talkative Indians. "Like they can't tell! Hey, Bet, why didn't you get coffee?" She told the others about the coffee-spewing at McDonald's, making a funny story of it, describing Vince, including Anthony, and soon they were all trying to outdo each other by telling their most embarrassing moments. Bernadette sent Nadine a grateful smile. She'd much rather they laugh at her than bicker among themselves. Complaining was no way to win.

When David told how he'd stood up to go to the men's room during a movie and gotten his belt buckle stuck in the hair of the elderly man in front of him, only the hair turned out to be a hairpiece, Bernadette laughed so hard, the waiter had to bring water.

"Hey, speaking of movies. Did anyone see *Stand and Deliver* on cable last week?" Lori asked.

No one had.

"It's about these poor Hispanic kids with this great math teacher who makes them take the AP Calculus test, and they score so high, the test people think they cheated." She took a ladylike bite of her chili dog. "I don't know why, but I thought of us."

Bernadette felt Nadine's worried glance at her.

"We're not poor," she said quickly. She'd promised—no more second-guessing.

"Or Spanish," David pointed out.

"And nobody thinks we cheated," Anthony said. "Unless you have something to tell us, Lori."

Bernadette had never seen anyone eat a chili dog without getting sauce on their fingers. But the pale green nails remained immaculate. "What I meant was," Lori said, unperturbed, "we're the underdogs."

"Oh, like U of M–Michigan State," Anthony said.

"Right," Nadine said with relief. "Which one are we?"

"State, of course. Working-class but spunky."

"Spunky" sounded like somebody's dog. Not to mention that, working class or not, Bernadette considered herself Ivy League material. But tonight she didn't quibble.

The talk moved from films to TV shows. To families, music, teachers, the upcoming dance, cars, colleges. They made so much noise, they'd have been thrown out of Creighton's local Big Boy, but the staff at Dmitri's didn't seem to mind. Maybe they were used to it. David drew amazing little caricatures of them all on the back of his place mat. Bernadette's cheeks grew warm, and she found herself smiling from the rare pleasure of having more than one person to talk to at the same time. If she could have traded that evening for another ride alone with Mr. Malory, she'd have had to think hard before choosing.

Finally Lori poured the last cup from their second pot of coffee. "I should get going. I told my mom I wouldn't be too late."

Anthony cleared his throat. "We need to talk about the reading list."

Constraint descended on the table. They looked everywhere but at each other's faces.

"I've been thinking—" Anthony paused. Everyone waited. "I've been thinking—videos."

"Videos?" Lori repeated.

"Yeah. Of the books. They're classics, right? I bet every one of them is a movie. That we can rent." His curly hair practically bounced off his head.

Bernadette held up her hand. "Hang on there." Based on the tape they'd just watched, Mrs. Phoebe Hamilton was indeed more interested in breadth than depth. Characters, authors, broad plotlines. And Creighton Community Library carried almost every series ever aired on PBS. Had anyone said they had to *read* their assignments?

They were all looking at her. "Videos might work," she said, and it seemed to her that a little sigh of relief went round the table.

As though she'd been waiting for just those words, Nadine chimed in. "Books on tape!"

"Abridged," Lori breathed.

"Cliff's Notes?" David asked.

"Excelente, amigo." Anthony pulled out his pen and began to make a list. "I'll be Primary on videos. My brother's friend runs a video store, we won't even have to pay."

"My neighbor is blind," David said. Everyone

looked at him. "For the books on tape! She gets them from the library for the blind—she says they have a great selection. And I do her yard work."

Bernadette sighed in relief, and even pride. They weren't quitters after all.

Anthony noticed her sigh. He always seemed to be watching her. "Did you think we'd give up, Ms. Terrell? Wizards like us? Tsk, tsk, tsk."

She only smiled. "Children's books," she said. "All those myths and Bible stories, and Shakespeare? They do them for kids." She looked at Lori. "Big print. Colored pictures. You'll like 'em."

"You mean, like, I have to get a library card?" Lori used two fingers to flick back her hair in good-natured self-parody.

Even as Bernadette laughed and glanced at Nadine with a shrug that said, *all right, so I like her,* she couldn't help feeling tricked. How could Lori *bear* to let people think she was stupid? Bernadette would sooner be a hunchback.

"Don't tell Malory," David ordered. "He thinks we're going to do this the right way."

David hadn't seen the Porsche parked in the handicapped space in the garage. Or Life Saver foil gone with the wind. "I wouldn't worry about that," Bernadette said.

chapter twelve

Stuff the head
With all such reading as was never read . . .
—Alexander Pope, *The Dunciad*

That was Thursday night. Friday morning David came up behind Bernadette while she was putting her books in her locker. "Pssst."

She jumped, and scraped her head against the top shelf. "Jeeze Louise, David." She rubbed her head and eyed him sourly. He looked like a cat who'd consumed an entire aviary.

He opened his binder cover an inch. "What do you think?"

"I can't see a thing."

He used the locker door as a shield from prying eyes. "*Now* do you see it?"

The comic book's cover showed a dark, sinister man on a horse looming over a terrified girl whose bosom was about to spill out of her skintight, laced-up bodice. One breast sported a big red "A."

"*The Scarlet Letter,* by Nathaniel Hawthorne. Classic Comix."

Bernadette's eyes widened, and a favorite saying

of her mother's ran through her mind: Even the great chefs use canned soup sometimes. She clutched David's arm. "Is this the only one you have?"

"Nope." He radiated smugness. "They only had five titles in stock. But they checked online, and it looks like we can get at least twenty more." Modestly he added, "I'm one of their best customers."

Bernadette pumped the hand of this short, handsome pervert she had clearly underestimated. "I've got to give you credit, David," she said. "There's Pinehurst up there translating *Beowulf* from Old English, and we're reading it in comics! And people think *they're* the geniuses!"

David's fair skin reddened. Bernadette Terrell was not known for handing out compliments. "Thanks, Bernadette. Hey, wait'll I show Anthony. He's gonna croak."

He strutted down the hall. Bernadette leaned against her locker and watched him. Well, well. *See,* she told the pesky voice of doom in her head. *We do have a chance.*

Other people agreed. The whole town had Wizard fever.

The *Creighton Courier* ran a front-page story with the headline "Wickham Wizards Out-Class Pinehurst Panthers." Martha Terrell bought copies for all the relatives, and Bernadette pinned one to her quote-board.

At Farmer Jack's seafood case a sign said, FISH IS BRAIN FOOD — ASK A WICKHAM WIZARD, with an arrow pointing to the *Courier* clipping. Bernadette felt like royalty until she found out the deli supervisor was David's aunt.

The Creighton public library filled its glass display case with a history of the NCS Classics Bowl. Martha gave them a freshman year photo in which Bernadette still wore glasses and bangs and could pass for twelve. Ms. K. denied influencing the librarians, though the display quoted her calling all the Wizards "remarkably passionate readers."

Still, support rolled in from so many places, it couldn't all be a setup. Mr. Tony's 10-Minute Oil Change on Grand River sent them coupons for free oil changes, and Mr. Tony was not related to any of them. The hospital's audiology clinic offered them free hearing tests ("the better to hear the questions"); The Book Nook sent ten-dollar gift certificates; a local cable station asked to interview them. After we win, Mr. Malory told them; his Wizards were busy.

Maybe parents wanted to prove that tax dollars could educate kids as well any pricey private school. Bernadette couldn't say. Her European History teacher claimed there was nothing like a common enemy to bring people together. Of course, Mr. Carlson had been speaking of the Allied Powers. But he could have been talking about Creighton.

***

Meanwhile, English class meant practice and more practice.

"What does the Ancient Mariner wear around his neck?" LaShonda asked.

Bernadette pressed one of the buzzers Mr. Malory had gotten the Technology Club to build. "An albatross."

Two desks away, Mitchell quizzed Nadine. "What god was forced to bear the heavens on his shoulders for all eternity?"

"Atlas," Nadine said as Bernadette's lips shaped the answer.

Across the room the other Wizards paired off with their non-Bowl classmates. Uncorrected term papers and ungraded quizzes piled up on the front desk. Under Mr. Malory's watchful eye, murmured answers to murmured questions floated in the air, punctuated by buzzes.

"Name the trilogy —"

"Who wrote the first —"

"From what country did the —"

"What miracle did Jesus —"

"Complete this stanza —"

After-school practices meant Scored Bowls. These were mock Classic Bowls with teams of two each, with the fifth person acting as scorekeeper. Mr. Malory made flip cards in ten-point increments just like in the Bowl tapes. From the red binder that grew fatter each week came questions and more questions. Within days they all had a thorough understanding of the scoring, when it paid to guess and when it was better to pass. Mr. Malory favored the guess. "We'll not win this by playing it safe," he said. "Don't miss points to preserve the opinion of *Pinehurst*."

Bernadette loved how he said it—as if to be concerned with Pinehurst was way, way beneath them.

During the second week of contest preparation, Bernadette opened *The Red Badge of Courage* at home—she was backup to Lori on Children's Classics—and a paper fell out of Chapter One. It was a cell phone bill, in Lori's own name. Bernadette paused an instant to envy Lori such luxury—catch Bernadette's mother giving her daughter a phone Martha couldn't listen in on—before beginning to read. Two pages later she stopped and unfolded the bill again. Three calls were to a phone number she recognized.

Mr. Malory's.

Odd. She got out the phone book and double-checked his number, but it was the same. Curiosity ate at her. Each call had lasted more than ten minutes—one had been twenty-two minutes long. What could be so urgent Lori had to call their teacher at home and talk for twenty-two minutes? Bernadette's imagination ran through scenarios that ranged from Lori being a secret stalker to Lori only *returning* calls Mr. Malory had made to *her* (this she dismissed as absurd—Lori was not his type), to the calls being made by someone else—Mrs. Besh, perhaps.

The likeliest answer was that Lori had questions about her Bowl assignments she was embarrassed to ask in class—yet even that seemed peculiar. Bernadette could think of no way to find out, short of asking her. (She did not even consider asking Mr. Malory.) For one thing, she'd have to admit she'd read the phone bill and recognized the number. But the real reason was, she was afraid to presume. Lori always treated her pleasantly and would probably tell her whatever she wanted to know, but that didn't mean Bernadette had a right to ask. She and Lori Besh were teammates. Not friends.

After practice one day (Nadine left so quickly, Bernadette missed her chance for a ride home), Bernadette waited in the media center for her mother to finish work and come get her. Ms. Kestenberg casually mentioned that she would soon be helping Mr. Malory with the Wizard practices.

Bernadette cocked her head at that. "Help?" she asked. "How come?"

Ms. K. was sorting through old magazines. "Evidently a close friend of his has cancer. Frank will have to be out a lot these next few weeks, and he knows I'm familiar with the books you'll be reading, so—"

"*Out* a lot? Out a *lot*? What about—"

"Just after school. He has to be in Ann Arbor in time for visiting hours, a few times a week."

"Oh." That must mean the U of M hospital. There certainly was a lot going on in Ann Arbor these days. Bernadette had lived seventeen years in Creighton and hardly noticed the place, yet suddenly the college town was popping up everywhere. "What friend?"

"Gene someone."

"Gene like a man, or Jean like a girl?"

"Gene like a man, and that's all I know, not that it's any of our business," Ms. K. said firmly.

Hmmm. "That's a lot of extra work for you, isn't it? What with debate, too?"

From a stack of back issues of *Causal Link—The Debater's Bible*, Ms. K. regarded Bernadette with misty surprise. Bernadette waved a hand in front of her face.

"Aren't you sweet to think of that! You know, Bernadette Terrell, you're a much nicer girl than you pretend to be. But I'm onto you." Ms. K. beamed at her fondly. "All that aggression on Saturdays during the rounds—that's just for show, isn't it?"

Bernadette wrinkled her nose in embarrassment. No, it wasn't.

Ms. K. laughed and bustled away toward the

ladder leaning against the Reference shelf. Rungs dipped beneath her weight as she climbed. "But don't you worry about me. Quizzing students on classics will do me more good than water aerobics. Usually what they want are the shortest books with the biggest print, or *worse*," she said with a disdainful sniff, "Cliff's Notes."

Bernadette trailed after her with guilty steps, an image of the study guides, cassette tapes, and children's books on her bedroom desk taunting her. She held the ladder steady while Ms. K. shuffled books on the top shelf, and when the librarian thanked her for her help she mumbled something about having to meet her mother outside, and beat a rapid retreat. Their shortcuts were perfectly legal, of course. But for a moment there she'd felt like a fraud.

The next day she stopped at Mr. Malory's desk after class. "Ms. Kestenberg told me about your sick friend, Mr. Malory. I wanted to tell you, I'm really sorry."

His lips tightened. "Thank you, Ms. Terrell. I hadn't realized Ms. Kestenberg would discuss my private matters with the students."

He was angry! "Ms. K. is a friend of mine. I don't think she knew it was a secret."

"It isn't, especially. But I dislike being the object of speculation. No matter how well-meaning."

He smiled then, but for once it failed to charm

her. Bernadette stammered out an apology and fled to the cafeteria. The object of speculation! She slapped her silverware down on the tray. As if every girl who passed him in the halls didn't speculate about being trapped in an elevator with the divine Mr. Malory. What he'd say, what she'd wear, how his kisses would taste . . .

Oh. Maybe that's what he meant.

chapter thirteen

He is an Englishman!
For he himself has said it,
And it's greatly to his credit,
That he is an Englishman!
— Sir W. S. Gilbert, *HMS Pinafore*

That week and the next, Bernadette read. When she wasn't reading she walked around with headphones on, listening to books on tapes. She stuffed towels under her door so her parents wouldn't see her light, and read so late that her eyes felt grainy and tight in the mornings.

During this period Martha Terrell championed any Bowl-related activity. She couldn't do enough for her daughter, even though, Bernadette thought guiltily, no one was asking her to do anything. Meals that had previously been hit-or-miss became ruthlessly nourishing. Meatloaf appeared, made with oatmeal and wheat germ and something rubbery that neither Joe nor Bernadette, exchanging baffled glances while chewing, had the nerve to ask about; spaghetti from whole-wheat pasta with spinach sneaked in the sauce; homemade waffles on a plate instead of Pop Tarts in the car on the way to school. Martha bought horse-sized

vitamins and waited while Bernadette choked one
down each morning. If Bernadette Terrell blew the
educational opportunity of a lifetime, it wouldn't be
from poor nutrition. Nor did Martha's considera-
tion stop at the kitchen. Whereas in former days
Bernadette's ability to lose herself in a book so that
she didn't hear ringing stove timers, doorbells, or
parental summonses had driven Martha wild, now
she tut-tutted and made Joe do chores instead. She
kept the TV volume low so as not to disturb
Bernadette's reading. She filled the gas tank, paid
off all outstanding library fines (which had been
riding for months, though Bernadette did not tell
her), and on the Saturday Bernadette was supposed
to clean out the garage but slept late instead,
Martha did it herself.

Even stuffed with stories and questioning her
own sanity in attempting what she saw every day as
an impossible task, Bernadette noticed. She was
touched. And a little unnerved. This red-carpet
treatment couldn't last forever, and then what?
Would Martha's kindness vanish if Wickham lost
the Bowl? Bernadette knew better than to ask. Her
mother's motives were like her meatloaf—best
swallowed whole.

And at the after-school practices, more questions.

Bernadette discovered that she looked forward
to these practices with an anticipation previously

reserved for a new Sarah Sloan. From these sessions, more intimate than a class and lasting longer than a debate, she learned more than books. She'd always thought of David Minor as just a lecherous, though accomplished, cartoonist. Now she came to admire the quiet doggedness that meant he never missed the same question twice.

She couldn't say the same about Lori Besh, who had a potentially fatal habit of only reading first chapters (though she could relate the plot of *Hope Springs Eternal* for the last seven years, so the problem was not with her memory). Yet Lori showed such a cheerful humility and, gradually, such an increase in her attention span, that Bernadette's ire melted. She did hope, though, that the Classics Bowl judges took their questions from the beginnings of books.

She even liked Anthony's terrible literary jokes. What American novel described St. Ursula's new uniforms? *A Farewell to Arms.* Yuk, yuk. But as time passed and the sessions grew steadily more tense, any laughs were welcome.

As the Wizards' exhaustion mounted, so did their resourcefulness. Inevitably, this showed.

When David was asked, "Name the three characters in *The Hunchback of Notre Dame* who represent good, evil, and temptation," he replied, "Quasimodo, uh, Victor, and Hugo," the last two being the gargoyles in the Disney movie.

Asked who defended Tom Robinson in *To Kill a Mockingbird*, Nadine said, "Gregory Peck."

And when Anthony had to name the sister who died in *Little Women*, he smacked his forehead with his hand. "One of them *died*?" he asked, and Mr. Malory's left eyebrow arched toward heaven. The tape had been on clearance and was only one cassette long, Anthony explained to Bernadette later. Naturally sacrifices had been made.

Ms. Kestenberg coached on, happily oblivious, but Mr. Malory *had* to know. Yet all he ever said was, "Get it right tomorrow." Circles had appeared under the green-gray eyes, and on occasion a note of impatience marred the silken voice. Bernadette pictured him sitting up late with his kitten, Sheba, inventing new questions to test his Wizards. This always filled her with shame and a fierce resolve to work harder. The man was a Trojan, a demigod. He was *willing* them to win, and didn't they want that, too?

At least twice a week he left the after-school practices early. Once, staring out the window and only half-listening to Ms. K., Bernadette saw the Porsche shoot out of the teachers' lot and head west toward 275.

Gene must be getting worse.

Nine days before the Bowl, Mr. Malory disclosed that he'd investigated the academic background of every member of the Classics Contest research committee. Reconnoitering, he called it.

"They choose the questions." At the front of the classroom he rubbed his palms together. "And this year's lot are Anglophiles. Hardly a Hemingway or a Faulkner expert in the bunch. A stroke of luck for us, don't you think?"

"What's wrong with American literature?" Bernadette knew she sounded peevish. She'd been up till midnight reading things like "When the mist was on the rice-fields an' the sun was droppin' slow/She'd git 'er little banjo an' she'd sing *Kulla-lo-lo!*" As far as she was concerned they could take Kipling and stick him where the sun dropped slow.

"There's nothing wrong with it," Mr. Malory assured her. "Much of it's quite readable. But in terms of world influence, well"—he gave a slight shrug, as though disclaiming responsibility for this well-known fact—"the English tradition dominates."

He stood as he did in her dreams, leaning back against his desk with his hands grasping the desk edge, one polished slip-on propped on the toe of the other to reveal several inches of faultless silk sock. The sun pouring in the windows was so strong, he'd rolled the sleeves of his white shirt to the elbow. With eyebrows arched in amusement he forced them, nicely, to acknowledge the superiority of English literature over any scribblings the New World had managed to produce. Only in this backwater Michigan school, his air implied, would one need to spell it out so bluntly.

Normally Bernadette enjoyed his urbane snobbery. But she was tired. "I *like* Emily Dickinson," she said stubbornly. "*And* Edna St. Vincent Millay."

He winced ever so slightly. "Of course. All young girls do." He threw her a forgiving smile and moved on.

Bernadette steamed to herself. That smile said she was a silly, romantic girl. Or maybe it said only girls liked women's poetry. Whatever it said, she didn't like it. What about Yeats? Browning? Hopkins? She liked them fine. What about the war poets—their lines reeked of blood and bayonets and limbs knife-skewed—and she'd been as moved as anyone. Mr. Malory had given her an A on that report, or had he forgotten? She was *not* a silly young girl.

She saw what had happened. He no longer regarded them as individuals. For him they'd all melted together into The Wizards. The Team. His weapon in the upcoming War of Words.

"Hey, Bernadette. Wait."

It was almost 4:30. The halls echoed emptily. Lori had vanished to pompon practice in the gym, and Nadine had just vanished.

Bernadette slowed to let Anthony and David catch up.

"Was Malory ragging you, or what?" Anthony

asked. "All young girls like Emily Dickinson, didn't you know? You'll grow out of it."

He did a wickedly good English accent. Bernadette gave a reluctant smile.

David held up his hand. "Do you hear that?"

Someone was screaming. Ahead of them the school's senior secretary ran shrieking across the hall.

"That was Mrs. Ivey!" David started toward the principal's office.

"Stop!" Bernadette grabbed his sleeve. "What if there's some nut with a gun up there?"

No one said "don't be ridiculous."

"Aah. I didn't hear any shots," Anthony said, staying where he was. Finally, moving together, they edged up to the corner and peeked around.

In front of the sign that read MAIN OFFICE/ VISITORS MUST SIGN IN, Wickham's principal was hopping from one foot to the other and flapping her skirt so that it billowed out wildly.

She saw them and shouted. "Get away! It's bees!"

Bees? Bernadette dropped her books and dashed across the lobby. Something zinged past her cheek. "Mrs. Standish, let's get out of here." Another zing made her smack her neck.

"I can't! There's one in *here*." Mrs. Standish plucked at her neckline and tried to peer down at her chest.

Bernadette fumbled at the principal's collar

buttons and soon released a furiously buzzing honey bee. It zoomed out to join five dozen relatives zipping around the lobby like ricochets from a drunken sniper. Then she dragged Mrs. Standish out the door and into the sun. "You have two stings on your face, with the stingers still in them."

"Is that bad?" Mrs. Standish was breathing fast, but she buttoned up her dress as though to partially disrobe in the school lobby was standard procedure.

Bernadette felt an unwilling flicker of respect. "It's not good. They should come out."

The principal stuck out her chin. The boys had followed them out onto the front steps, and now they drew closer to watch. Bernadette reveled in the heady sense of being in charge. This must be what doctors felt.

Spic 'n' Span had skin the texture of too-often washed satin that might tear any second. Bernadette scraped out the stingers and showed her the tiny black dots. "Got 'em. You should just put a little baking soda and water on your face and . . . wherever else they got you. It'll help the itching."

"Oh," Spic 'n' Span said on a long note of pleased discovery. "Baking soda! That's what my husband used once when he got stung up at our cottage. Baking soda. Hmmmph." Her fingers patted the sting sites as though they were controls to a time machine into the past. Behind her glasses her eyes went soft and distant.

"Or meat tenderizer," Bernadette added.

The principal's faded eyes focused sharply on her. "Thank you, dear. You've been very helpful." She straightened her shoulders. "Katherine, call an exterminator," she ordered the still-sniffling secretary. "Tell them it's bees." She gave a little shudder. "Filthy things."

To David and Anthony, still hovering nearby, she said, "I'll need you boys to move the furniture out of my office. We'll have the whole place sprayed immediately."

"Wh-what about the bees?" David asked.

"Now don't be nervous Nellies," the principal said. "Take the screens out of the windows if you're scared of a few stings."

Bernadette hastily volunteered to hunt up some baking soda. She walked the silent halls and chuckled at the memory of the principal dancing with bees. Strange or not, Spic 'n' Span was one tough cookie. You had to feel sorry for the bees.

There had been a long, darned tear in the principal's slip. Bernadette's smile turned thoughtful. How much could a slip cost?

"It makes you think," she told the rows of lockers. It really did.

If the school board did decide to give a bonus to the principal when she retired, Bernadette Terrell would not object.

chapter fourteen

She got tired of thinking aright; but there was no serious
harm in it, as she got equally tired of thinking wrong.
In the midst of her mysterious perversities
she had admirable flashes of justice.
—Henry James, *The American*

The next day the Wizards had no practice.
Four-thirty saw Bernadette stretched on the living
room couch with a bowl of caramel popcorn on
her stomach and the TV volume on high. All this
Bowl cramming was cutting into her *Jeopardy!*
time.

On the screen Alex said, "The seventeenth-
century writer whose most famous work was com-
posed in the dark, so to speak."

The front door slammed. "I'm home!" Martha
called.

"SHHHHH! Milton," Bernadette said to the TV.

The returning champion's light went on. "Who
was Shakespeare?" she asked.

"Sorry," Alex said.

"Milton!" Bernadette shouted.

"Who was John Donne?" a second contestant
guessed.

Alex shook his head.

"'In the dark,' imbecile! He's *blind*!"

The third contestant didn't even guess. Bernadette bounced popcorn all over the couch. "Who was John Milton! I can't believe the idiots who get on this show!" Then, "Hey there," she said more mildly.

Martha had come up beside her. Now she pressed "mute" on the remote control. "Did you forget that tomorrow is your father's birthday?" she asked with ominous calm.

Bernadette sat up at once. Her mother must have had a bad day with a waiting room of behaviorally challenged teens. "How old is Daddy?" she asked brightly.

"Forty-six. You forgot, didn't you? Like you forgot to practice the violin for the last two weeks, and to feed the fish, and where you parked at the mall. You with the photographic memory."

"I told you, that's just for printed stuff," Bernadette said. So the honeymoon was over. In a way, this return of the normal Martha was reassuring. A person liked to know what to expect. "Can I use the car tomorrow?"

"If you pick up the cake."

"Be glad to." Bernadette longed to turn the sound back on, but her mother wasn't finished.

"Honey, are you okay with all this studying?" Still in her coat, Martha sat down on the coffee table. "It isn't too much for you?"

"It's *fine*."

Martha's lips tightened knowingly.

"Mom, it's only one more week. It's *ten thousand dollars*! Isn't that worth losing a little sleep over?"

Her mother picked up some stray kernels and dropped them in the bowl one by one. "Maybe. Maybe not. I'll be glad when it's finished, that's all. Your team might lose, you know. And then won't you feel silly."

"Oh! Oh! And when one of your patients commits suicide," Bernadette sputtered, "do the counselors feel *silly* for trying to save them?" This had happened the year before. Her mother had been devastated.

Martha's look withered her. "The Classics Bowl is not life and death. It's just a contest."

She stood up and left before Bernadette could think of a suitable reply. Just a contest! "And Olympic gold is just metal," Bernadette said to a mute Alex. Talk about blowing hot and cold! Who would screech the loudest if Wickham lost to Pinehurst? Martha Terrell, that's who.

Bernadette's spirits rose every time she entered Borders Books. It was as soothing as church. Classical music played in the background, good coffee and cocoa fragrances wafted from the little café, and thousands of vividly colored books whispered, *Read me*. Usually she wandered the aisles for an hour before realizing she'd forgotten what she came for, her head was spinning, and she desperately needed the bathroom.

But today she made straight for cookbooks. Her father loved the electric bread machine he'd gotten for Christmas. But three months of Basic White had his daughter hungering for a change.

A whole shelf on bread machines. Amazing what people would write entire books about. *Bread Entrées, Bread for Left-Handers*. She settled cross-legged on the carpeting and immersed herself in *Miracles to Make in Your Bread Machine*. She was wondering whether Chinese Black Bean and Garlic Rolls would be interesting or vile when a voice above her said, "Hi." Giant sneakers appeared by her knee.

She raised her head. Anthony Cirillo looked different today. Ah. The smirk was missing.

"Hi," she said.

"Your dad told me you'd be here."

Luckily she was already on the floor. McAss had called her? "Here I am."

"Uh—you want something to drink?"

"If you're buying." She got to her feet. "I love hot chocolate."

He grinned, and looked more like Anthony. "What, no coffee?"

"Gave it up for Lent," Bernadette said. "Along with brussels sprouts and milk of magnesia."

Over tall mocha-caramel lattes (extra whipped

cream for Bernadette), Anthony said, "I wanted to tell you something. You know how Spic 'n' Span had us moving furniture yesterday?"

Bernadette nodded. Who could forget The Sting?

"After we moved some file cabinets, she went somewhere—I think the bees shook her up more than she let on. Turns out they were in the bathroom drywall—the exterminator said the hot weather wakes them up. So anyway, David and I are moving everything out when I see this one cabinet with a drawer marked RECOMMENDATIONS." He stopped.

"And?"

"So I figured maybe teachers filed recommendations of students there—a reference file so they don't have to think up lines like 'works to capacity' and 'shows good leadership skills.' You know?"

"If you don't hurry up I'm going to pour this on you."

"Okay, okay." He took a breath. "It was a file of recommendations *Spic 'n' Span* wrote, for teachers who had applied for other jobs."

Bernadette stopped rushing him.

"She wrote one for Malory. To Pinehurst. Last August."

"Impossible," she said.

"It was a decent reference."

"But he's still here!"

Anthony stared into his cup. "I know."

They sat there and thought the same thing. *Mr. Malory got turned down by Pinehurst.*

The whipped cream tasted cloying and thick in Bernadette's throat. Anthony was watching her with something dangerously close to pity in his eyes. That would never do.

"Well, of course he'd want to teach somewhere else. Who wouldn't? Wickham's a dump." Her voice rose. "Kids at Wickham think *The Way of All Flesh* is a dirty movie! The cafeteria smells like armpits, the art trailer's from World War II for God's sake, and they have bees in the bathrooms! Malory would have seen right off that the place is full of losers."

Mr. Malory had wanted to teach at Pinehurst? Inconceivable.

Anthony sipped his drink in silence, which enraged her. *She* had plenty to say. "Who the hell does Pinehurst think they are? I bet they'd turn down Jesus Christ—tell him his Shinto background was weak."

"Malory knows his stuff," Anthony agreed.

Bernadette eyed him suspiciously. If he added, *too bad he's gay*, or *it's a shame he talks like a wuss*, she would punch him. Right here in Borders.

Watching her as though hoping she was armed only with a spoon, Anthony said, "Maybe that's why he wants to beat them in the Classics Bowl."

"Revenge? What's wrong with that?"

"Nothing. It doesn't mean he doesn't really think we can beat them."

Bernadette worked that out. "But you think it does," she said slowly. "Don't you. You think he's fooling himself, and us right along with him."

Anthony raised his hands as if to say *not so fast.* "I want to hear what *you* think. You're the Wizard with the memory." His hand came across the table-top to touch her own for a fleeting second. His skin was warm. "I'm not trying to pressure you. It's just—man, we could use that ten thousand bucks."

"Who couldn't." She thought furiously. So Mr. Malory had an excellent reason of his own to resent Pinehurst. How coincidental. How—surreal.

"No, I mean it. I don't know if you know. . . ."

Some awkwardness in Anthony's voice made Bernadette stop pondering the implications of this news and look over at him.

"My brother's my legal guardian. Our dad died when I was little, and our mom—she died two summers ago." He addressed his knuckles. "That's why Vince isn't in college—he's going to put me through, then I can put him through, if he doesn't buy up a bunch of Mickey D's before then. Ten grand that we don't need to pay back would help a lot."

"Oh, Anthony." Bernadette set her cup down with a thump. "I'm so sorry. I didn't know." *Why hadn't* she known? A person being an orphan was not a national secret. Some detective she would make.

"It's all right. I thought maybe Nadine might have said something. . . ."

"I haven't seen Nadine much lately." He must know why. She felt off-balance, ashamed. And as though she should repay him for entrusting her with something so personal.

Abruptly she said, "I don't care about the TV part."

"What TV part?"

"Looking stupid on cable TV. That doesn't bother me." Bernadette had never confessed this even to Nadine. She kept her head down over her cup so that her hair formed a curtain between them. "What bothers me is that we could lose by some huge margin because we have such a horrible background in the classics. It'd be different if it was the Cartoon Bowl. But it's not. We're trying to cram years of reading into one month. Lori and David petrify me—they think I'm so smart. You know how you just said I'm the one with the memory? Well, that's the thing. *That's all I have.* But Pinehurst—" She shook her hair back and met his eyes across the table. "Anthony, you have no idea. They've got people who are *truly* smart. Who know what these books *mean*, why they're worth reading. This one kid on their team? Nadine and I debated him once, and he quoted *Voltaire*—and I don't mean as a first affirmative. I mean on the fly. Needless to say, they won."

There. It was out, her humiliating secret, and apparently all Anthony Cirillo could do was stare at her hair. When it dawned on him that she'd finished talking, he shook his head with a frown of disappointment. Bernadette's stomach twisted inside.

"This isn't about IQ!" he said. "This is about work. You think NCS wants us to prove the theory of relativity? Hell, no. We depend on you *because* of your memory. Debate logic won't matter in this thing. What'll count is how much we've managed to stuff in our brains for one hour. The rest'll be luck. You want to worry about something, worry how fast you can push a buzzer—not how smart you are. Or aren't." He had a grin like his brother's, and Bernadette suddenly saw how a person could find that attractive. "If people want to give me prizes and money because I have a good memory, let 'em. *I'm* not stupid."

"No, I—I never thought you were."

"And if you're worried that your memory will give out, don't be. It never has before, has it?"

Only when certain people wore collarless shirts. "No. . . ."

"As for David and Lori—yeah, they do think you're smart, but so what? It's a common mistake. I've been known to think it myself." He rolled his eyes in disbelief, but his smile held new assurance, as though her confession had pleased him in some way.

He must be using something different on his skin. It didn't look as terrible as it used to. Flustered, Bernadette said, "Did you tell David about seeing the recommendation?"

"No. He was out in the hall."

"Good. Don't. If the other Wizards thought Mr. Malory was in some kind of grudge match, they could get all upset."

"Not like us," Anthony said blandly. "Whatever you say, Captain. I barely got the letter back before Spic 'n' Span came in. She gave us little packs of Lorna Doones for helping her."

"Lorna Doones?"

"Yeah. She had a whole drawerful. I think she's got a thing going with the vending machine guy."

Bernadette giggled. Anthony had not so much as blown a straw wrapper across the table this whole time. He could have made a snide remark about Nadine and Vince, but he hadn't. Her gaze fell on the bread book. "I should get going."

"Me too. I gotta check out the Cliff's Notes."

"Don't spend too much."

Anthony was shocked. "I never *buy* them," he said. "I read them here."

"Oh. Well, thanks for the drink."

Bernadette paid a teenaged clerk for the book, which he seemed to find very funny. Since when was bread funny? *She* wasn't laughing at his nose stud. Back in the car she adjusted the rearview mirror and discovered that the ends of her hair wore a coating of whipped cream, as though they'd been dipped. She swore softly as she cleaned it off.

Still . . . Anthony hadn't seemed to mind.

chapter fifteen

Friendship is constant in all other things

Save in the office and affairs of love . . .

—Shakespeare, *Much Ado About Nothing*

Her father loved the bread book. Bernadette phoned Nadine after church on Sunday while munching a piece of warm Jalapeño Corn Loaf.

Nadine was out.

Bernadette scowled at the wall. Nadine was out a lot these days.

She should be back by dinner at the latest, Nadine's mother told Bernadette, as Vince had to work the evening shift. "Which is a good thing if you ask me."

"What is, Mrs. Walczak?"

"That he has to work *sometime*. I don't trust this big rush—dinners out on school nights, sending her roses, the whole bit. He reminds me of a Robert DeNiro movie."

"*Taxi Driver?*"

"No, I don't think he's insane." But she sounded doubtful, as though Bernadette had suggested a new and plausible theory. "The ones where he plays those Mafia types."

Bernadette considered this. On first impression, Vince did have a kind of underworld savvy, but thinking he might be a hood was like thinking Nadine should know how to plant rice. "You really think the mob runs McDonald's, Mrs. Walczak? That would be some cover."

"That's what my husband says." Nadine's mother sighed. "Don't have daughters, Bernadette. Have sons. They can't get pregnant."

Bernadette did not point out some of the things they *could* do. After she hung up she wondered what it was with mothers. All they thought about was sex. Nadine had known Vince for only two and a half weeks.

Parents watched too much TV.

Bernadette didn't expect it, but Nadine called back.

"Hi." She sounded cool.

"Hi yourself. What's up? How's Vince?"

It was the magic question. "Oh, Bet! He's great. We just got back from seeing *Farewell My Concubine* downtown. It's Chinese."

"*That* must have been fun."

"It was. Not the movie, though, that was sad. Vince thinks I've been denying my heritage."

"As a concubine?"

"As an Asian."

"You're not Asian," Bernadette exclaimed. "You learned to talk from *Sesame Street* like everybody else."

"I know, but I *look* Korean."

Did Nadine look Korean? To Bernadette she just looked like . . . Nadine. "You know what Kipling says: 'Oh, East is East and West is West, and never the twain shall meet.' You'd be the East," she added.

"Thanks. Wasn't Kipling the one who called Gunga Din a squidgy-nosed idol? I don't care what he says. Vince thinks being Korean is something special."

"Uh-huh. Does Vince speak Italian?"

"Just a few swear words."

"*That's* special."

"I don't expect you to understand."

Her superior tone goaded Bernadette past endurance. "You want to know what I understand? That you're so busy researching your damned heritage at McDonald's that you're not reading your list. We're all worried sick."

"Who's 'we'?"

Uh-oh. "Lori said something."

"Lori Besh is worried about *me*?"

"Yeah. And David. He's worried."

"David." Nadine's voice dripped skepticism.

"Yes. And—and Ms. K. is concerned. She never sees you in the media center anymore, she says. *Nobody* ever sees you anymore."

"Oh, Bet." Nadine's sigh was so adultly conde-scending that Bernadette considered stuffing the portable phone down the garbage disposal. "Tell them I'm reading my share and then some. And then tell them they should think about getting a life. I gotta go." She hung up.

Bernadette stared unseeingly out the window over the sink. Nadine hadn't asked why she'd called. Not that Bernadette had planned to worry her by telling about Malory being turned down by Pinehurst. But Nadine hadn't even given her a chance to be tempted. She had just assumed Bernadette wanted to hear her go on and on about Vince Cirillo, when in fact it all made Bernadette slightly ill.

Asian movies! Nadine Elaine Walczak was about as Asian as a Baby Ruth bar.

Her parents came in from shopping before she could finish brooding in peace. Martha set down her bag of groceries with a loud thump, looked at the phone in Bernadette's hand and the expression on Bernadette's face, and said, "I told you this would happen."

"Don't start. I'm warning you." Bernadette stood stiffly while her father came over and mas-saged her shoulders.

Martha said no one was starting anything but these things always happened when your best friend fell in love, and the wonder was that it hadn't happened sooner, and so on, and so on, until Bernadette escaped upstairs.

It was easy for her mother to talk. She had a husband who for some reason thought her wonderful. A block full of neighbors, the people at work, clients and their families who needed her . . .

Bernadette had only Nadine. Who'd never said a word about roses.

That night Bernadette came downstairs only when she was sure her mother had already gone to bed. At the kitchen table her father pored over papers from his job. She settled in a corner of the couch with *The Grapes of Wrath.* They read in companionable silence.

By 11:30 the Joads had another flat tire and she couldn't keep her eyes open. "I'm going to bed."

"Come here just a minute, would you?" Joe Terrell patted the chair next to him. "Pumpkin," he began awkwardly.

"Hmmm?"

"I just wanted to say—don't let your mother upset you. You know. That business about Nadine and her boyfriend."

The phone call came stinging back. Bernadette's mouth turned bitter. "It's hard not to get upset, when I ask her to leave me alone and instead she gives me a lecture. Like it's *my* fault."

Her father took her hand in his. The lamp hanging over the table made his gray hair—when had it gotten so gray? Bernadette wondered—gleam silver. "That's just her way. Your mother thinks talking things over is therapeutic—even if she's the only one talking. I was glad you didn't make a big scene about it." He cleared his throat. "She's going through the change, you know."

Bernadette thought he'd caught Martha rifling through the box of quarters on his dresser.

"Mood swings, hot flashes," he continued. "I read a thing in *Reader's Digest* on it. That's why she's so cranky these days."

Oh, that change. "I can't tell any difference."

He chuckled softly. "You're your mother's child, all right."

Bernadette grabbed his hand and pressed it to her cheek. "No, I'm not. I'm yours."

"You've got the best of both of us in you." He hugged her. "I never worry about my pumpkin."

"Oh, Daddy." She hugged him back, then turned the letter he'd been reading toward her. Paper-clipped to it was a page from a store catalog. "Who's sending you pictures of luggage?"

He snorted. "Some guy in Redford claims this set of brand-new suitcases, among other things, was in his basement when it flooded—wants us to give him the full replacement value."

"Does he have the receipt?"

"What do you think? He doesn't even have the suitcases. Says they smelled too bad, so he threw them out. And he forgot to take photos."

"So what do you do?"

"I tell him very politely that the evidence won't let us give him the amount he's asking—you never call customers liars—and I pay him the fair market value on used suitcases. That's all his policy covers. He'll get more than he deserves, we'll be slightly cheated, and it'll be business as usual." He patted a pile of paper beside the letter. "I got six more claims here, and what do you want to bet five of them overstate their loss. If there *was* a loss."

"Wow. Does everyone cheat?"

"Oh, no. One time a client sent *us* a check—she found her diamond ring in the bathtub drain, so she was returning the insurance money. Now that was a day. The branch manager bought me lunch on that one." He grinned, remembering. "But mostly it's lies. Penny-ante stuff. My customers could never be politicians, they don't steal big enough." He massaged his neck tiredly.

"Do you like this job, Dad? Because it sounds awful to me."

His smile was so full of love and pride, it made her throat ache. "I'll tell you what I like. I like watching my daughter practicing up to be a *Jeopardy!* champion so she can win her parents a vacation to Europe." He ruffled her hair. "Did I tell you Grandma wants me to tape the Classics Bowl for her? She's going to show it to her euchre club. You'll be the talk of Manistee." He looked at the kitchen clock. "What are you doing up so late? You can't win anything if you're tired. Go to bed."

Bernadette climbed the stairs through sudden tears that stung her eyes. That insurance job sounded like something even the Joads would turn down. And her father was so sweet. It wasn't fair. While her mother—well, Bernadette was fast coming to believe there was no accounting for taste. Look at Nadine.

chapter sixteen

If there were no girls like them in the world,
there would be no poetry.
— Willa Cather, *My Antonia*

The next day was Monday. At lunch, Bernadette and Nadine ate with Lori and pretended that everything was normal between them. At least Bernadette pretended. Maybe Nadine really thought things *were* fine, which just went to show how little attention she was paying these days.

Out the window they saw Mr. Malory get into his car and drive away. He wore sunglasses.

"He's gorgeous," Nadine said dreamily.

Bernadette stiffened. "You've got a boyfriend, remember?" she said coldly. "You want to be careful or you'll get your fantasies mixed up."

"Who says they're fantasies?" Nadine smiled mysteriously while Bernadette tried in vain to think of a scathing reply. "It's like I just got a brand-new VW Bug. Suddenly I see VW Bugs everywhere, and I have to compare them to mine. What do you think, Lori? Does that make sense?"

"I don't think you should talk about Mr. Malory like that."

Bernadette and Nadine looked at each other, surprised. Lori frowned at them. "You make him sound like some—some centerfold. If he hadn't done all that research, we wouldn't have a prayer against Pinehurst. It's just not very—respectful."

"I'm *very* respectful—especially when he wears that gray shirt with the button open. C'mon, Lori, I'm only kidding." Nadine coaxed, but Lori wouldn't smile.

She'd called him "drop-dead sexy" not three weeks ago. From force of habit Bernadette found herself exchanging glances with Nadine, who didn't even know about the cell phone calls. What was happening here?

After practice that afternoon, Nadine couldn't give Bernadette a ride home. Errands to run, favors for her mother, etc. The usual. She said this fast, gathering up her books, with little sidelong glances that dared Bernadette to object.

Bernadette would eat worms first. After Nadine's showing off at lunch, she'd be damned if she gave the Korean Kid another chance to tell her to get a life. "Don't put yourself out," she said. Lori glanced from her to Nadine. "I'll call my mother."

"I go right down Grand River, Bernadette," Lori volunteered. "I'll give you a lift."

"Thanks, that'd be great." Bernadette ignored Nadine's wink and "how about that" face. Maybe Nadine wanted to pretend they shared some secret about Lori, but secrets were precisely what they did not share. Not lately.

Lori had parked on the far side of the track. The summery weather from the week before was still in evidence, and the March day had soared into a temperature range Michigan did not normally feel until June.

Bernadette ambled across the football field. With each breath of balmy air her worries about best friends, contests, and faculty members with perplexing secrets baked away in the physical joy of hot sun on her face.

Track season had not officially started, but a few members of the boy's team were wrestling hurdles into place over by the far goalpost. More boys raked the long jump pit. Lori stopped to watch three girls practice the shot put.

These were seniors, serious-faced and solid as tree trunks in their dark green Wickham sweats. They went through an identical series of moves: warm-up stretches, a practice rotation, then the actual throw. Numbered markers in the field made it easy to gauge the distances.

What Bernadette knew about track and field she could put in her eye and not even blink, but even to her this crew didn't look much of a threat. That last toss barely cleared twenty-five yards. It appeared to have given its thrower a cramp, because she fell to the ground swearing and clutching her side.

Lori went over and said something. The seniors exchanged looks. One of them snorted. Lori dropped her backpack and slipped off her pompon jacket. Her silver hoop earrings glinted in the light.

Sly grins passed between the shot-putters. Bernadette sat down on the track. This ought to be good.

Lori's short pleated skirt and cap-sleeved sweater suggested Miss America being photographed at a construction site. Her hair flamed red-gold in the sun. Muscles Bernadette herself did not own flexed in Lori's upper arms as without self-consciousness she did some elbow-behind-the-head stretches. Right, left, arms behind the back. The sweater grew taut. Over by the long jump pit all motion ceased.

The seniors' grins turned thoughtful.

Lori took up her stance and faced the back of the scuffed dirt circle. She tucked the shot snugly under her chin. She leaned backward on one bent leg, took two little hops in a turn, then exploded skyward like a released metal coil. Her shoulders twisted as she thrust the shot forward and grunted the "ooof" of a sumo wrestler.

The sequence imprinted itself on Bernadette's brain: Lori frozen in time, her muscled arm stretched out before her, a vision of power and grace whose beauty caught at the throat.

The shot thudded down past the thirty-five-yard mark.

The seniors were as shocked as if it had landed on them.

"Thanks, guys." Lori picked up her things and strolled back to Bernadette.

"That was awesome." Bernadette scrambled upright and trotted behind her. "You smoked them. You blew them away! You are in the wrong sport, Lori Besh."

Lori's composure dissolved into flattered giggles. "I've tried it before, once or twice. I used to date a shot-putter."

"Date one? You are one!" Bernadette tripped over her words. "With your SATs and a *real* sport like track and field, you could be Ivy League material. U of M, anyway. Scholarship City."

Lori gave a crow of laughter. "Ivy League? You're nuts. My SATs *might* get me into Michigan State."

"What, a 720 on Verbal? That's excellent."

"I wish. I got 520 on each part. What's the matter?" Bernadette had stopped. "It's not that bad."

"Of course not. 1040. It's fine." Bernadette resumed walking. "It's just—you said once you were good at tests. I thought you might have aced them, that's all."

"I did ace them. I got 1040. Why'd you think I had a 720 on Verbal?"

"I must have been thinking of somebody else."

"Yeah, like yourself."

"780," Bernadette said automatically. It wasn't like Mr. Malory to get things wrong.

"780! Get out." Lori's admiration was pleasant, Bernadette could not deny. "If I ever scored that high on anything, my dad would fritz out but good. He thinks I'm a dumb blonde—without the blonde."

This jolted Bernadette back to her companion. "But—I thought your father was dead."

"That's what I tell people," Lori said. "It's just that he *should* be dead."

Bernadette couldn't believe it. She waited, on the off chance that this was a bad joke, explained any second. But no. Lori met her eyes steadily. She wasn't joking.

They had passed the wooden bleachers and come to the trip wire separating playing fields from the graveled parking lot. Lori stepped on the wire for Bernadette.

"Thanks."

"I'm not a liar," Lori said.

"Of course not."

"I'm the daughter of a liar, but I don't think those things are genetic, do you?"

"No," said Bernadette, a parishioner in good

sacramental standing at St. Jerome's. "Lying is an act of free will. Otherwise it can't be a sin."

They reached the little red Miata, but Lori made no move to get in. "My mom divorced my dad two years ago. Turned out he had a girlfriend. You want to know the worst part?"

Bernadette wanted nothing less, but Lori needed to tell. Even she could see that much. "What?"

"He had her for five years before we found out. Since I was ten. She lived in Farmington." Farmington bordered Creighton to the west.

"Really? We went to this great Thai place once in Farming—"

"We never caught on. He missed my dance recitals, and gymnastic meets, and one time three days of our vacation, and we just thought, oh, he's snowed in in Denver again."

"Did he ski a lot?"

"He's a pilot. When he *was* home he slept half the time. My mom thought he was anemic. She couldn't figure out how he could keep flying with such iron-poor blood." Lori gave a twisted smile. "I get my brains from my mom, can't you tell?"

The smile did it. Bernadette's heart contracted at its bravery. If Mr. Besh had appeared at that moment she would have swung her backpack into his cheating crotch with every ounce of her strength.

Lori went on. "He had these old albums from college he used to rave about—Spooky Tooth, Little Feat, groups you never heard of that he always swore were collectors' items—and the day my mom told me about Glor—about the divorce, I went upstairs and sailed those albums out the window. My mom and I had a contest—who could get theirs the farthest. I won. She hated him more, she said, but I had the better arm." Lori made a wry face.

"You have a great arm." Bernadette couldn't think of anything to say. Clumsily she patted Lori's shoulder. "Your dad was some kind of sick."

"Oh, yeah. He's one screwed-up puppy." She looked into Bernadette's face and asked, as though she really thought Bernadette might know, "How can a person you think you love, who's supposed to take care of you, look you right in the eye and lie? Year after year . . . and to my mother! I get so mad even now, I could—oh, I don't know. It's over." She kicked at a patch of gravel, which hit the tires with impotent thuds.

"Poison him? A letter bomb?" Bernadette suggested. "Or wait, I've got it—acid. Blind him so he can't fly."

Lori gave a startled gasp of laughter. "I used to think about running away from home just so he'd feel guilty."

"What! Lori, listen to me." Lori obediently fastened her blue gaze on Bernadette. "*He's* the bad guy.

Not you. You want to do something, do it to *him*. Like the albums out the window—that's the idea. I know Jesus says turn the other cheek, but then how can you be sure people get what's coming to them?"

For a long moment Lori stared at her. Then she broke into a rippling laugh. Bernadette was pleased. "Now why couldn't that dumb counselor have told me that? She just kept saying to 'deal with my anger.' I like your way better."

Bernadette coughed. "You do realize, I'm not actually suggesting—"

"Don't worry. You're kidding, I know, but I appreciate that, too. I didn't mean to go on and on." Lori pressed the unlock button on her key ring. "Anyway, we did great in court. I think of this car as a present from Dad." There was no anger in her voice, only a philosophical self-mockery. "The SAT scores made me think of him. He got the highest grade on the airline's entrance exam of any pilot they ever had. I used to be so proud of that. But now—" she made a face— "he probably cheated."

"Lori—"

"Do me a favor? Forget I mentioned this."

"Absolutely."

They got in. Lori put the car in reverse and carefully backed out. The silence felt awkward. "What's your mother do?" Bernadette asked, and held her breath in case Mrs. Besh turned out to be a kleptomaniac, or a porn star.

But Lori smiled. "My mom's Miss Tanya."

Miss Tanya's School of Ballet had been a fixture in downtown Creighton as long as Bernadette could remember. "*I* took lessons from Miss Tanya when I was four," she cried.

"No kidding? I took them about a hundred hours a week."

"Do you still?"

Lori's face wrinkled into distaste, as though there was something uncool about dancing. This, from a devotee of pompon, struck Bernadette as funny.

"I mostly just teach," Lori said. "Beginning ballet three nights a week and twice on Saturdays."

"*And* pompon, *and* study for the Bowl? God, Lori. It's a wonder you're not sleeping in class."

"My mom's taking my night students this month. She knows what the Classics Bowl means to me."

They turned off Grand River into Bernadette's subdivision. Lori glanced over at her. "You'd think I'd want to win it for her, wouldn't you? And I do. But what I really want is to win, and take the computer or the check or whatever they give us and shove it in my father's face. *Look at this,* I'd say. *I'm smart enough without you, I don't need a father.*" She laughed at herself. "Is that dumb or what."

Dumb? Suddenly Lori's phone calls to Mr. Malory made some sense. He was kind and he was around. Compared with Mr. Besh he must look like the father on *The Brady Bunch*. "I don't think it's dumb," Bernadette said.

She turned toward the window and made a quick, hidden sign of the cross. *Jesus, Mary, and Joseph. And Saint Bernadette, too, if you're listening. We have to win. Please.*

chapter seventeen

... then he seized his left foot with both his hands in
such a fury that he split in two ...
— The Brothers Grimm, *Rumpelstiltskin*

On Thursday — Bowl Day Minus Three — Bernadette
slumped at her desk in the classroom grown familiar as
a cell and listened to her stomach rumble.

Two desks away, Lori yawned. Bernadette
yawned back. Nadine yawned, too. David had his
head down on his arms and hadn't moved in some
time. Anthony came in. He dropped his books
with a bang that made them all yelp.

"Hey, Ms. Terrell." He leaned toward her and
lowered his voice mysteriously. "I have something
you'd love to get your hands on."

Bernadette stifled a yawn. "What?"

Anthony waved his notebook. "The genuine,
actual questions for this year's Classics Bowl. Get
'em while they're hot."

Bernadette jerked upright so hard, her neck
twinged, shooting a fiery pain toward her ear.

"You *do*?" Lori twisted around. "I don't believe
it. Read some."

Bernadette catapulted out of her seat. She grabbed at the notebook, but Anthony backed toward the blackboard holding it over his head.

"Bet, he's lying. He doesn't have them." Nadine's gruff voice held amusement.

"Oh, yeah?" Anthony said. "Listen to this—"

"NO!" Bernadette screamed. Was he crazy? If he read them out loud, it was over. Everything would be over. She leaped up again.

Anthony fended her off as though she were a puppy. "Name the Laura Ingalls Wilder classic— ow!—about an elf who carries a tent camping," he shouted.

Huh?

"Little House on the Fairy. Get it?" Anthony's laugh was a bray.

Bernadette's arms dropped to her sides. Her heart hammered painfully. "That wasn't funny."

"Well, it was, kind of. How did you think I'd get the real questions?" he asked her. "Kissing up to Phoebe Hamilton? She's a little old for me."

"And still in her right mind," Nadine put in.

David jotted something down. "I have one. Name the English novel that describes Anthony at work."

"Well, *Animal Farm*'s American." Nadine made a hideous face at Anthony. "So it must be *Lord of the Flies.*"

"Ooh, ooh. Let me try." Lori ran a silver finger- nail down her book list while they all waited.

"Okay. What English novel describes the Wickham Warriors' halftime show?"

Nobody knew.

"Middlemarch!" she cried. "Get it?"

Groans from all around, but Lori settled back in her chair with a very satisfied expression.

Bernadette recovered from her scare. This was a competition, after all. "What did Tarzan say when his girlfriend put a plastic bag over his head?"

"Jane—Air?" David guessed.

Bernadette whistled. "You're quick," she said, and earned one of David's louder burps.

It was as though Madison Avenue had announced a prize for the worst pun. They couldn't stop themselves.

What did you call a residence with HBO in every room? *House of the Seven Cables.* What did the hammer say when he took the remote control away from the pliers? It's *The Turn of the Screw.* What did they call Johnny Bench when he retired to New York? *The Catcher in the Rye.*

"These are worse than my cousin's joke books. And he's only six." Nadine scoured her book list. "Okay, okay. Gimme a good name for a bathroom sink store."

"Vanity Fair!" Bernadette yelled.

At first no one noticed Mr. Malory. He stood in the doorway with a pink box under one arm and a black scowl on his face. Bernadette, who could sense fresh doughnuts through stone walls, looked up. So did David.

"Hey, Mr. Malory," David called, leaning back on two chair legs. "What did the waitress say when the guy ordered a martini?" He answered himself immediately. "'Olive or twist?' Get it? *Oliver Twist?*"

"I 'got it' all the way from the main hall, Mr. Minor. Let's hope your knowledge is more impressive than your wit." Their teacher's voice was clipped and cold and burningly sarcastic in a way they'd never heard it.

David's chair legs crashed forward. Anthony folded himself into his desk. Lori laced her hands in front of her, kindergarten-style. Through the open seatback of Bernadette's chair, Nadine's foot prodded her in the ribs like old times.

Mr. Malory looked them over as though they were something a plunger had brought up. He unlocked the file drawer in his desk and took out the familiar red binder. This he opened with great deliberation. "Ms. Besh," he said. "Suppose you tell us who wrote the *Lyrical Ballads*."

Panicked blue eyes sought Bernadette's. "I can't think—" Lori stammered.

"Ms. Walczak?"

"Coleridge and—Byron?"

"Coleridge. And. *Wordsworth!*" He smacked the desk top. "Coleridge and Wordsworth, only the most influential poets of the Romantic period." He rifled through his papers. "Who had Romantic Poets?"

Everyone started leafing through their assignment packets as though they had to check.

"Ms. Besh."

Lori squeaked.

"Do you see Romantic Poets on your assignment sheet?" he asked with dangerous softness.

"I guess I didn't get to them yet, Mr. Malory."

"And when *were* you planning to get to them? Between cartwheels, perhaps? Or were you hoping to ink a few names on your arm the day of the Bowl?"

Lori looked stricken. Bernadette shut her eyes.

Then opened them. She could split Romantic Poets with Lori. "Mr. Malory, what if I—"

"No." He hurled the doughnut box the width of the room. It thwacked against the doorjamb. "The bloody *hell* with this. Do you think I've done all this work so you can act like a bunch of asses?"

No one answered.

"I've not given up my afternoons *and* evenings *and* weekends for the pure pleasure of your company. I had hoped you would rise to the challenge. That you'd feel you had something to prove. But obviously I've been kidding myself." He slammed the binder shut. "Pinehurst Academy knows how it feels to be winners. Perhaps if you ask them nicely on Sunday they'll describe it to you."

He strode from the room, giving the door a good bang behind him.

Bernadette stared at the bent box of doughnuts, its poor sugary contents squashed and spilling out, and suddenly time warped and she was ten years old, shopping with her mother at the grocery store.

Bernadette had waved a coupon in one hand and a box of doughnuts in the other. "'One Free Coffee Cake, Any Flavor. Not Good on Doughnuts or Sandwich Rolls,'" she recited to the cashier. "So these don't count, Mom."

Martha had laughed airily and said, "Well, what were you supposed to do when there weren't any coffee cakes left?" But the cashier stood there as stolid as lard and did not offer to make the swap and finally Martha said, "Oh we'll take them, anyway." When they got out to the car she lit into Bernadette like nobody's business.

"Let me explain something to you," she'd said as she slung a gallon of milk on top of the lettuce. "Food companies want us to buy their products, right? So when they're out of one thing they want us to buy something *else* they make, why do you think I *go* to that cashier who God knows is slower than Christmas. Understand?"

Bernadette understood they'd be lucky if one egg out of twelve survived. She had nodded, solemn-eyed.

The mix of anger and righteousness in her mother's tone that day—she'd just heard it again. In Mr. Malory's voice. The doughnuts brought it all back.

Her fellow Wizards came out of their trances.

"What set *him* off?" David asked, aggrieved.

Nadine snapped her fingers. "He's lost it. Gone postal."

Lori sniffled back tears. "It's all my fault. He gave me a chance, and I messed up. I am *so* sorry."

"Sorry?" Anthony leaped out of his chair with a crash. "Did you say you're *sorry*?" He swept to the front of the room and began stalking back and forth, waving his arms like Mussolini berating the troops but sounding more like Winston Churchill.

"Do you think I'm in this bloody contest for my health? Do you think I've neglected your grammar, ignored your essays, not even opened the practice tests that just might help you all pass the AP exam next month," he removed an imaginary pair of glasses, mimed folding them and putting them in his shirt pocket just the way Mr. Malory did, "and treated your mediocre classmates as though they were pond scum, just for the bloody *fun* of it?"

Bernadette gasped. She looked behind her at Nadine, but that was a mistake. Giggles racked them both, helpless little snorts that turned into hiccups of hysteria. It was so awful, and so true.

Anthony bowed. He got a second wind and ranted on about the bloody this and bloody that, retrieving the crumpled pink box and strafing them all with doughnut holes as he paced up and down.

Lori sniffled to herself. But Bernadette, cramming still-warm glazed bits of dough into her mouth as though they had medicinal value, breathed more freely. Anthony was always a clown. You could depend on him.

The door opened.

Anthony stopped in mid-rant.

It was only Ms. Kestenberg, in a suit so turquoise it shimmered. "Mr. Malory is quite upset," she said, and held up her hand against their clamor. "It isn't you. His friend Gene—the one who's been so sick?—he died this afternoon."

They fell silent. As an excuse for bad behavior, death was hard to beat.

Nadine and Lori murmured, "Oh, no!" while David and Anthony shrugged in uncomfortable, manly forbearance. The guy's buddy had kicked it, no wonder he was bummed.

Bernadette rejected the last cake doughnut hole and chose a coconut-covered mutant. She chewed thoughtfully. She had seen plenty of movies where people died—she knew what grief looked like. Certainly death might make you angry.

But would losing a loved one make you mean? Put a cagey glint in your eye, make you pick on people who didn't deserve it? Well, yes, it probably would. But would it let you buy doughnuts as though they still mattered?

Call her cold-hearted, but something felt off.

That night the temperature plunged into the thirties. The wind roared in the streets, blowing words around and around just too fast for a listener to make sense of.

Bernadette closed *The Prelude*. Out her bedroom window tree branches lurched in a wild dance. Overdue homework sat heaped on her desk, and downstairs her parents discussed her in worried tones. Tonight she would dream of pages of type so clear, she could name the fonts.

The wind shrieked and moaned in a language she didn't speak, yet it seemed to have a message for her. She shivered and returned to her reading. Whatever was making the skin on her neck prickle, it wasn't coming from any book.

chapter eighteen

O Hamlet! What a falling-off was there.
—Shakespeare, *Hamlet*

Bernadette half-expected Mr. Malory to take the next day off. But Friday morning there he was at his desk, wearing his gray shirt, her favorite. A bit casual for visiting a funeral home, wasn't it?

He fixed his gaze somewhere over the tops of their heads. "I owe some of you an apology for losing my temper yesterday."

The non-Bowl students looked curious at this, while the Wizards made polite pooh-poohing noises. It was nothing, he'd been upset, anyone would have been annoyed at how silly, etc.

Lori's complexion had a sallow tinge, and the blue eyes were bloodshot. "I know Romantic Poets," she announced.

Bernadette quailed. *Don't start him off again.*

Mr. Malory considered Lori. "Do you, indeed?" he said. "Let's try you, shall we?"

He flipped open the red binder. "Name the

161

poem Wordsworth wrote that was inspired after the death of his daughter."

"'Surprised by Joy,'" Lori said.

"In the following verse, what is the poet describing? 'Ten thousand saw I at a glance/Tossing their heads in sprightly dance.'"

She didn't hesitate. "Daffodils."

"In *Christabel*, Coleridge introduced a new poetic technique. Instead of counting the syllables in each line, what did he co—"

"Accents!" Lori cried joyfully.

"Splendid, Ms. Besh. Well done." So must Gepetto have gazed upon Pinocchio.

The whole class applauded. As an omen for the Classics Bowl it couldn't have been bettered.

Lori's pleasure put color back in her cheeks. "Oh, stop," she said, and ducked her head. "They were on my *list*."

But she couldn't stop smiling, and Bernadette would have confessed to poor study habits before revealing that she, too, had stayed up until far too late steeping herself in the Romantic period. Just in case.

At lunch Nadine happened to mention, looking out the cafeteria windows, that since practice was canceled she thought she'd leave after fifth period to make a stop at the mall. She did not invite Bernadette.

"Sure." Bernadette supposed she should be thankful Nadine still ate lunch with her. "It won't kill me to take the bus home."

"Bet—"

"What?"

"Nothing." Then, helplessly, Nadine said, "You think everything is black and white. All one way or another. You know? You're so—so *intense*."

Bernadette stared at her. Then she drained her milk. Pushed back her chair. "Yeah. It's part of my charm. Catch you later, crocodile." She had to blink very hard on the way to the conveyer belt, where she sent her tray down the line bearing an untouched piece of coconut-cream pie.

Of course she was intense. Intense was good, it was tough-minded. Intense was an achievement. If Nadine wanted a wimpy, "anything you do is fine with *me*" friend, she could just look elsewhere.

She did, said the little voice.

In fifth hour Mrs. Standish came on the PA system. "Please join me in extending our best wishes to Mr. Malory's team of Wickham Wizards, who will take on Pinehurst Academy this Sunday"— boos echoed throughout the building—"in the National Computing Systems Classics Bowl. It will be carried live on Channel 28 at five P.M. Tune in and watch our Wizards win!"

On her way into the media center, Bernadette

was stopped once again by the ring-in-the-navel girl. The ring wasn't visible today, but the short blond hair had turned magenta.

"Hey, Bernadette," she said.

Bernadette had found out her name, too. "Hey, Samantha."

"You gonna beat Pinehurst?"

"Gonna try."

"Good. I think Wickham taking them on is the coolest thing ever. Make 'em cry, okay?" She gave Bernadette a thumbs-up gesture.

Someone would be crying Sunday, of that Bernadette was sure. She only hoped it was Pinehurst.

Ms. K. sat at a study table, reference volumes stacked all around her. Her suit glowed yellow as a Yield sign.

"Hi, Ms. K." Bernadette set her books on the table and sat down. "Um . . . is something wrong?"

"Bernadette, I want an honest answer."

"Okay."

"I caught David Minor reading this—this *thing*. Did you know about it?" In her hand was an especially lurid comic book of *Tom Jones*. If the woman on the cover showed any more cleavage, she could advertise for a topless bar over in Windsor.

Bernadette leafed through it, stalling for time.

"Racy stuff, Ms. K. You should be ashamed of yourself."

The librarian did not smile. "I want to know if the whole team has been using these rags to study for the Bowl. Have they?"

"Um—maybe. A little."

"Bernadette!"

"Not *much*. Only when we're the backup in a category."

"Really?"

"Really." Mostly.

Ms. Kestenberg flicked a page with her fingernail. "They shouldn't even sell these. All that's here is the plot, bits of it, and suggestive cartoons."

"You should see the PBS video," Bernadette said without thinking.

"Video?" Ms. K. asked with fresh horror. "You're watching *movies*?"

"To remind us." Bernadette tried not to sound defensive. They hadn't broken any laws. "You've seen our assignment sheets, Ms. K. How could we read all that in one month?"

"Does Frank Malory know?"

He had to. Bernadette looked into Ms. K.'s troubled eyes. "I didn't tell him."

"It wasn't his idea?"

"Oh, no. It was ours."

Ms. Kestenberg heaved a sigh of relief. "I knew he wouldn't condone this. Not the way he respects learning." She dropped *Tom Jones* in the waste-basket, then lifted a fat volume from the table and began to ascend her ladder. The public schools Accreditation Committee was due soon, and the library would come under scrutiny.

"Hand me volume three, would you please?"

Bernadette got out of her chair and handed up volume three. "You know what I think, Ms. K.?"

"Yes, I do. You think I should be happy your team is reading anything at all and not out spray-painting filth on the principal's car." Ms. K. climbed higher. The ladder creaked. "You didn't hear about that? No, never mind what they wrote. Volume four, please."

Bernadette hoisted up volume four. Ms. K. stretched to place it on the highest shelf. The ladder tilted to the left. "I like to think the Wizards are different, Bernadette. They're studying literature, works of—AAAHHHHHH!"

She gave a wild whoop and clutched the ladder in a death grip, her red mouth a perfect circle of distress. Bernadette tried to pull the ladder back to the center but it was like trying to snatch the license plate off of a speeding car: Ms. K. soared along the Reference shelf like a large and terrified canary.

The floor shook.

"Oh, God." Bernadette dropped to her knees. Every student in the place rushed over. "Ms. K.? Ms. K.? Are you all right?"

On the carpet the librarian looked small, curled in a ball and cradling one wrist. She opened an agonized eye. "Help me up, Bernadette."

The emergency room was packed.

"An ambulance would have seen that median strip," Bernadette insisted.

"I told you, it's all right. I was already in pain." Under her smooth layer of foundation Ms. K. was an interesting shade of whitish-green, with lines of strain showing around her puckered mouth.

Bernadette looked at the clock on the ER wall. Two-forty-five. They'd been here one hour.

"More ibuprofen?" she asked. "My mom says you can take four before you damage your kidneys."

"I'm fine, Bernadette."

But anyone could see that she wasn't.

Finally the clerk called Ms. K.'s name. A nurse ushered them into an examination cubicle. Ms. K. asked Bernadette to stay and she could not very well refuse, though she'd rather have read the scribbled-on *Highlights for Children* in the waiting room.

A young man came in. His white coat said DR. PAI, but he didn't look much older than Anthony. Bernadette hoped that meant he was especially brilliant.

He manipulated the wrist, now swollen to

twice its normal size. "Does this hurt?" He pressed on the bone.

"YES," Ms. K. roared. "It hurts like hell because it's *broken*."

"I believe you are correct." Dr. Pai quickly withdrew his hand. "But still, we will require X rays."

Another nurse produced a wheel chair, and Bernadette jogged behind it to Radiology. In the hallway Ms. K.'s head lolled back against the chair. *So much for feeling fine,* Bernadette thought miserably. Suddenly Ms. K. jerked herself upright. "The cat!"

"What cat?" Bernadette glanced around. She saw lab technicians, empty gurneys, acres of linoleum—but no cat.

"Frank's cat. I'm supposed to take care of it while he's out of town. It makes noise if it's left alone too long." Ms. K. stroked her wrist, puffed up now like a python with a pig in it. "Oh, dear. I don't think I'll be driving for a while."

"Out of town?" Bernadette yelped. "What about the Classics Bowl?" A passing nurse glanced at her.

"Shhh. He'll be back Sunday," Ms. K. said. "I'm sure it has to do with Gene."

This was carrying grief too far, in Bernadette's opinion. Out of town! What if he crashed his car, or missed his plane? What about the Wizards?

Ms. K. was watching her. Ms. K. thought she

was much kinder than she actually was. Bernadette liked that in Ms. K.

"I could get the cat for you," she offered now. "I'll pick it up and take it to your house."

"Oh, that would be wonderful. You know, Bernadette, I think I'll take some of that ibuprofen now."

Ms. K. gave her Mr. Malory's address, which she pretended to need, and his apartment key, which she really did. Assuring Ms. K. she'd be back as soon as she got the cat, Bernadette set off on her second errand of mercy that day.

chapter nineteen

It would have made a cat laugh.
—J. R. Planché, *The Queen of the Frogs*

Bernadette found the Creighton Arms with the ease of one who'd spied on it a dozen times. Fearlessly she parked Ms. K.'s boat of a Buick in the spot reserved for 207-A.

In the tiny lobby her sense of adventure suffered a setback. Sunlight winked off a shiny brass plate: NO PETS ALLOWED.

Oh, if that wasn't Mr. Malory all over. How was she supposed to sneak a cat past every picture window in the place, including no doubt the landlord's? Adrenaline pumped through her at the idea of outwitting invisible eyes.

She got back in the car and cruised the complex until she found a rear entrance. She parked in front of a smelly Dumpster and prayed it wasn't trash day.

Someone had propped open the building's back door with a chunk of wood. Yowling echoed through the second-floor hall as though an angry baby had dropped its pacifier. "It's that Malory brat again,

Harry," the neighbors probably said. "Damned it if doesn't sound just like a cat."

207-A. She unlocked the door, slipped inside, and then shut the door quickly behind her, throwing the dead bolt for good measure. A furry weight struck her in the knees. The yowling—much louder in here—switched to low throated purring as the cat rubbed itself along a human leg. Bernadette could swear she saw surprise in the greenish-gray eyes that stared up at her.

"Oh, you big, sweet baby! I won't hurt you." She knelt down and put out a hand to be sniffed.

The cat's ears were outlined in dark brown fur that contrasted dramatically with the cream-colored rest of it. Its tail was enormous, long and bushy, and waved around like a weathervane. "You pretty thing, you," Bernadette crooned, scratching behind its ears. Those eyes reminded her of something. Where had she seen—oh. Mr. Malory's cat had clear, questioning eyes like its owner.

She started to pick it up, but it spit at her and shot away.

"All right, play hard to get." She stood up. "I'll just look around." Ms. K. probably hadn't even gone into X ray yet.

So this was the holy of holies.

The centered throw pillows on the sofa, the neatly labeled folders on the desk hutch, the hint of Pine-Sol—all evoked the immaculate interior of the

Porsche. Had it only been his academic credentials, or had Spic 'n' Span recognized the obsession of a kindred spirit when she'd hired Frank Malory?

Bernadette tiptoed across the carpet with Sheba a shadow behind her. The sense of adventure that had gripped her the moment she'd stepped into Ms. K.'s car grew stronger. Even the new, distracted Nadine would squeal when she heard Bernadette had seen Mr. Malory's sofa. Not that she was snooping; she was observing.

On the stereo rack an answering machine blinked its red light. She wouldn't *dream* of playing it. *That* would be snooping. He expected Ms. K. here, didn't he? She wouldn't do anything Ms. K. wouldn't do.

A louvered closet door just off the kitchen gave more testimony to a cleaning fetish. It held a tiny stacked washer and dryer, ironing board and iron, broom, dustpan, and a Dirt Devil vacuum cleaner.

Sheba grew bored and went to sun herself on the cat perch hooked onto the front windowsill. Bernadette eyed the sturdy wooden shelf. Surely that was deliberate flaunting?

Ah, well. She wasn't the judgmental type. Meanwhile, Ms. K. would certainly check out the kitchen.

Mr. Malory apparently survived on Rice-A-Roni, Royal Treat tea biscuits, and coffee. Bernadette used the dish cloth to open the freezer door so as not to leave fingerprints. Inside was a split-personality collection of Budget Gourmet dinners, Häagen-Dazs ice cream, and generic orange juice. Generic orange juice! For a man who could recite entire sonnets from memory! Life was not fair.

Still, envy pierced her. What joy to eat whatever you wanted, with no one to nag you to eat more, or slower, or sooner than you felt like. What *freedom*.

Would Ms. K. poke around anywhere else? She might have to use the bathroom, Bernadette decided. No one could object to that.

Sheba followed her like a conscientious realtor. The pine scent was stronger in the bathroom, clearly to cover up any trace of the litter box next to the sink. The sight of the box reminded Sheba of a pressing need, and Bernadette wrinkled her nose as the cat scratched daintily.

Two toothbrushes in a holder (his spare toothbrush was pink, how funny), a hygienic stack of paper cups, Ivory soap, sadly worn green towels. Nothing here worth reporting. The shower curtain concealed store-brand shampoo sitting next to a fancy salon conditioner. This unexpected vanity in Mr. Malory touched her, though Bernadette felt he really ought to save his money—this stuff didn't tame his wiry hair one bit.

She was out in the hall when a flash of color made her step back inside and swing the bathroom door away from the wall. On a hook hung a filmy, ribbony nightgown. A matching robe. And a navy blue brassiere.

Bernadette gaped, especially at the last item. Her own bras were optional affairs in white cotton. Drab, sturdy mules compared with this Pegasus of a garment. She reached out and fingered the fabric. Sheer, fine lace trimmed satin cups of an illicit softness. Size 34B. A phrase swam up out of memory. ". . . a college professor who models lingerie part-time." Who said that—oh, that had been Lori, inventing a suitable match for Mr. Malory. Bernadette's heartbeat checked again. Could these belong to—? Sanity returned. Lori Besh hadn't bought a 34B since sixth grade.

Her arm dropped. Mortification roiled her stomach like turned milk as the pink toothbrush, the fancy conditioner, and expensive ice cream took on new significance. *She* had fantasized romantic encounters with Mr. Malory. But those fantasies, shrouded in mist like the time shifts in *Brigadoon,* always faded out in a kiss prompted by a shared passion for the Western canon. She'd never dreamed of underwear.

Her skin burned from pictures she couldn't dismiss. She walked back into the living room and forgot for a moment why she was there. The cat padded past her and leaped onto the window perch.

"All right, so his sister's in town," Bernadette told it. "Or some cousin of Gene's." There would be matching panties, silken . . . "Probably too poor to get a hotel room." That was not the bra of a poor person. "Staying on the fold-out couch. She'd need something dark under mourning, it only makes sense . . ."

A cream-colored paw stifled a yawn—or was it a snicker?

"I bet he's at the airport right now—what is your problem?" Sheba was clawing at the picture window, uttering frantic baby-in-distress yowls.

Bernadette checked her watch. Four-fifteen— probably the time Mr. Malory normally came home. She had read stories about animals with amazingly accurate internal clocks.

She glanced out the front window.

And screamed.

The Porsche was in its parking slot. Below her the lobby door slammed, and familiar footsteps mounted the stairs two at a time.

She'd snooped in his bathroom. Felt someone's bra. Bernadette's cast-iron excuse for being in Mr. Malory's apartment became criminal trespassing.

Outside, a floorboard creaked. She lunged for the broom closet, slipped inside, and eased the door closed. By squinting between the slats she had a clear view from the window on her right to the stereo stand against the left wall.

A key turned in the lock, and the front dead bolt released with a crack. Frank Malory came in, tossed his key ring and books on the couch, and began to unbutton his shirt.

Oh dear God. Bernadette's heart skittered like a pneumatic drill. He stood at the desk in profile to her, undoing each button with a leisureliness that was pure torture. She squeezed her eyes shut.

She couldn't stand it—she looked. The gray shirt hung open to reveal the undershirt beneath, but apparently he'd thought twice about stripping in front of the window. He was rummaging around on the desktop and talking to Sheba as though resuming a long-running conversation.

"Ah, here they are." He put a small manila envelope into his back pocket. "A smart kitty would have made sure I had these this morning. What good are you?" The cat gave a happy meow and rubbed against his pant leg.

Keep talking, Bernadette prayed. Keep moving around, keep making noise. She couldn't budge. If she backed up one inch, the ironing board would knock against the wall. A thought paralyzed her. What if he'd come back to put on a clean shirt? A shirt that needed *ironing*?

"Sheba, you never said we had a message," Mr. Malory said reproachfully. The click of the answering machine was followed by the whir of a tape rewinding.

"Frank, it's me," a woman's voice began. "I missed you at school, so in case you're stopping home I wanted to tell you I'm running way behind."

"Me" sounded slightly breathless, self-assured, with a non-Michigan inflection that made Bernadette think of ivy-covered walls in New England towns. Me sounded—pretty. "I had to fax some last-minute stuff to NCS. If you get this, come straight to my office, I've got my things here." A low laugh, and the confident voice turned arch. "Including a few you've never seen. Bye now."

Bernadette writhed. *She'd* seen a few of them.

"A bit of luck, that," she heard. Then the rapid punching in of a phone number known by heart. "Dr. Fontaine, please." A pause. Sounds of plastic CD boxes being restacked. "Gena? Frank."

Gena?

"You're not the only one running behind. I forgot the tickets, believe it or not. But those opening acts go on for hours. Look for me in, oh, forty-five minutes, with luck and no police." He listened a moment, then laughed. "Yes, me too." The receiver clicked into place.

Footsteps sounded down the hall. A bang right behind her, like a doorknob hitting a wall, nearly made her yell. Her closet shared a wall with the bathroom.

She considered sneaking away. Then realized he'd left the bathroom door open. He would hear her.

She wiggled her toes inside her shoes while her English teacher answered nature's call for what seemed like an eternity. It didn't matter. She could stand it. Nothing was too awful, as long as he didn't catch her.

Her thoughts whirled around like moths trapped in the closet. NCS? Gena. Gene. Strange. Maybe Gena was Gene's twin sister. She certainly wasn't Mr. Malory's. Though she hadn't sounded very mournful. Nor did "opening acts" suggest any funeral rites Bernadette had ever heard of.

At last water surged through a pipe two inches from her head. Beside her came an insistent *beep, beep, beep.* Her digital watch glowed: four-thirty, time for *Jeopardy!* She fumbled for the alarm off button while sweat broke out on her forehead. A few seconds sooner . . .

On the other side of the wall a medicine cabinet clicked open. A bottle was unscrewed, screwed closed again, the cabinet banged shut. She heard the distant clink of hangers on a rod, then a sliding sound as though he was pulling the closet doors closed.

Her own door rattled before her face as though someone was trying it, and her heart jerked in a painful spasm. An ankle-high shadow bumped against the louvers, then purred.

Brisk steps rounded the corner from the hall. "Get away from that cupboard, now, and give us a kiss." Twelve inches from her legs, Mr. Malory scooped his cat up in his arms.

The almond spice scent of fresh Intrigue drifted through the door. "A very nice lady will be by — heavens, any minute now — to give you a little holiday. I told her you're a good kitty, so don't make me out a liar." He leaned over the back of the couch to pick up his keys. "Bloody hell!" he said. Sheba hit the carpet with a plop, and mewed in outrage.

Mr. Malory straightened up with the fat red binder in his hands and a relieved look on his face. "Talk about *in flagrante delicto*. Now where can we hide this?"

Bernadette tilted her head to see better. Eight months in his class had exposed her to the more basic Latin phrases. Talk about caught in *what* act? Why did he have to hide his Bowl papers?

He crossed over to the desk. Whistling under his breath, he took down a large blue binder. "I can't see Lucy peeking in Car Repairs, can you, puss? Recipes, now, that would be a different matter." He chuckled as he slid the red binder inside the blue one, and replaced them both on the hutch.

In the dark, Bernadette glowered.

He picked Sheba up and turned to scan the room. Two pairs of greenish-gray eyes stared straight at her, then slid past. Evidently satisfied, he picked up his keys, tossed the cat onto the sofa, and whipped the door shut behind him. The dead bolt sprang into its socket.

He was gone.

Bernadette counted to fifteen. Then to fifteen again. Not until she heard the muted roar of an engine did she push open the door.

The underarms of her good spring jacket were soaked. If he hadn't spritzed on aftershave, he'd have smelled her panic.

"Thank you, God, thank you, thank you, thank you." She tottered to the desk chair and collapsed. Sheba jumped up and kneaded her lap with soft, insistent paws.

"You!" Bernadette said. "You're a fine friend. If you could talk you'd have ratted me out in a second. Thanks a bunch."

She ran her hands over the soft cream fur. The steady throb of the warm, living motor gradually calmed her own breathing to normal.

On the desk hutch Car Repairs beckoned like Pandora's box.

She didn't even pretend Ms. K. would do such a thing. She had the binder open on the desk before Sheba could meow at being dumped.

The first page started her heart hammering again.

Bernadette knew that loopy writing from a thousand evidence cards. "*Name*: Nadine Walczak. *School*:

Wickham High." One hundred rows of five boxes each. An answer sheet from the Classics Contest they'd taken. Not the original—a copy.

She turned it over with fingers that shook. Anthony's sheet was there, and David's. Lori's. Her own. Here was the bootleg test itself, with its dire empty threat: IT IS FORBIDDEN TO COPY THIS TEST.

Bernadette Terrell had scored an eighty.

Not an eighty-seven. She counted up the circled wrong answers just to be sure. There was a calculator in the top desk drawer. The five scores averaged seventy-five.

Bernadette felt for the desk chair and sat down. She'd been right after all about someone cheating. Just wrong about who it had been.

Her mind jumped back to the day they had taken the test. It became a video camera, replaying the scene in slow motion.

She had finished first. Anthony next, then Lori. After a while Mr. Malory had gone out—to copy the test, he'd told Ms. Kestenberg. And obviously, she saw now, to cheat. He'd probably kept these copies as a record of what the team would need to learn. How had he known how many answers to change before Wickham's performance went from impressive to suspect? She didn't know, but he'd gauged it just right—at least for NCS. Then back to the classroom and his carefully selected proctors: one who thought he walked on water, and one who just hoped that wherever he'd been, he'd washed his hands.

The famous Terrell memory had not mattered at all. Frank Malory could make a Wickham Wizard out of a chimp.

That hokey explanation about normalizing— how could she have swallowed that? She groaned out loud. Every feeling revolted.

Sheba stared up at her, and she glared back. "So what?" Bernadette growled. "So someone cheated. Surprise, surprise." If she could live with the idea a month ago—and she'd managed to—she could live with it now.

But now it was Mr. Malory.

She choked off that train of thought immediately. There was no time to have hysterics all over the man's apartment just because he turned out to be a lying, cheating, sleeping-around manipulative BASTARD—

She turned over the test. Underneath it was a letter on University of Michigan letterhead. A photocopy.

Dear Research Committee Members:

As I mentioned in my fax, Mrs. Hamilton felt that this year's questions underrepresent British poetry. Your contributions (attached) will certainly remedy that. We feel that correct responses in the sixty to seventy percent range would be an excellent performance from this age group.

Thank you for your prompt response.

The typed name read "Genevieve L. Fontaine, PhD, Chairwoman, NCS Classics Contest Research Committee." The blue signature scrawled above it said "Gena."

It was dated March 17, twelve days earlier. At the bottom of the sheet bold black capitals warned: DO NOT CIRCULATE OR COPY.

Gene wasn't dead. He was a girl.

Under the letter were questions on poets from Auden to Yeats. The Wizards could answer them all. *Had* answered them, in bits and pieces, over the last two weeks. Her insides shriveled. All their practice this month, all those hours—it had been an act, to fool them into thinking that they'd earned The Power.

Some power. Their coach had the *questions*.

Bernadette wrapped her arms about herself tightly and bent over in the chair. Blood rushed to her head, and dark colors exploded behind her eyes, but she stayed that way a long time, rocking. *There was a crooked man and he had a crooked smile.* A beautiful, crooked smile.

After a while she sat up. She slid the binder back in its place. Now what?

She gazed around the apartment. She could take a kitchen knife and gouge dirty words on his CDs. Scoop the clumps from the litter box and hide them in his pillowcase. Pour Pine-Sol into his orange juice. He deserved all that and worse.

But she didn't do any of it. At that moment she knew about him, and he didn't know she knew. Years of Sarah Sloan kicked in. You might not know why or when you'd need it, but having surprise on your side was always an advantage.

Bernadette fetched Sheba and the cat supplies and locked up. By now Ms. K. would think she'd crashed the car. She banged her way down the stairs and out the back door, not caring who saw her. An illegal cat was the least of her worries. When she set the carrier on the ground to unlock the car, she checked her watch. Her life had changed, and *Jeopardy!* was still on.

chapter twenty

I do perceive here a divided duty.
— William Shakespeare, *Othello*

•

Whatever they'd given Ms. Kestenberg for pain made her so dopey, she didn't notice how long Bernadette had been gone. Bernadette helped her and her new plaster cast into the car, drove her home, and unloaded her and the cat. Then she called Martha for a ride. Her mother was so impressed by this Good Samaritan role, she forgot to scold Bernadette for not calling sooner.

That night, alone in her room, Bernadette let the implications of her discoveries crash around her.

Mr. Malory had cheated. If they won the Bowl it would be a giant scam. He'd set the Wizards up. And oh, one more thing—she was a fool.

She stared with loathing at the full-length mirror on the back of the door. Her eyes showed dull and pinkish behind the glasses she wore at home, as though she had a cold. Her flannel Harvard sleepshirt could stand a washing. "You even *look* kind of stupid," she told the mirror girl. "Easy to trick."

Clues that had been in plain sight all along shone now as though viewed through a special night-scope. The job reference to Pinehurst that Anthony had seen; the "missing" scoring procedure; Mr. Malory's lie about Lori's SATs; that thing he'd said in his car before their first team meeting, about how even if they had gotten in the Bowl by mistake that they could win with hard work — he had no doubt of it, he'd said. Well, no wonder. His arrogant belief in the superiority of English literature; the way rules didn't apply to him.

"And don't forget the flattery." She paced about the room, determined to flay herself with all possible recrimination. *Tell me I can win and I'll believe anything.* Mr. Malory hadn't wasted soft words on Bernadette Terrell about her eyes, her hair, her distracting legs. He had praised her mind. Said this was her year. Told her she could have The Power. She remembered the physical thrill she'd felt in his car when he brushed her leg, and hated him for that, too.

Abruptly she snatched up her purse from the desk. Zipped in the inside compartment were the matches she'd stolen on that drive. Gena probably had some just like them.

Bernadette bent back the cover and lit them all. They flamed to life in one bright, smokeless burst.

She held the book until it burned down to her fingers and then dropped it in a china mug.

Cheater. Liar. Betrayer. She ran out of epithets. He was all of those, but what was she?

A sucker? Or worse?

True, she had questioned the contest results. But she'd managed to stifle her doubts. "To win," she said out loud. "For *him*." She stopped in front of the door again. The mirror girl's left eyebrow lifted. "Oh, all right. And for Nadine. And my parents. And part of me wanted to win, too." Quite a big part. The faces of the other Wizards filled her mind's eye, their expressions intent and serious the way they'd looked during practices. David, Lori. Anthony. They'd worked so hard!

And now? Was Bernadette supposed to let her team walk into a setup? They called her Captain. They trusted her.

She couldn't do it. Frank Malory could sleep with the whole female faculty of any college he chose, she decided. He could catch every disease there was going (and the sooner the better), but he had no right to cheat his students. She felt as besmirched as if he'd turned out to be a child molester. Although, she had to admit, this was not *that* bad. But it was bad enough.

She went to bed and, eventually, to sleep. The stakes of the contest had changed. But it was still a contest—and Bernadette Terrell still hated to lose.

✳✳✳

At Creighton City Park the next morning the wind gusted cold and sharp. Even a headband and gloves didn't keep the chill out.

Bernadette jogged along the path that circled the park, narrowly avoiding a pile of dog droppings that belonged, at a guess, to a Saint Bernard. They had signs all over the park telling owners to clean up after their animals, but some people evidently felt *their* dogs' messes were a privilege to step in. She tied her hood around her face. When she turned to jog back, Nadine was coming toward her.

Her spirits rose. "Hey there."

"You look like a drug pusher." Nadine's breath came out in little puffs of smoke. Her jean jacket had no hood to disarrange her new swingy, geometric haircut. She wore earrings Bernadette had not seen before—little pewter pigs. "What was so urgent you couldn't tell me on the phone?"

"Excuse *me*," Bernadette said. "Am I keeping you from an Egg McMuffin? Or, wait, what's it called—kim cheese?"

"Kimchi," Nadine corrected loftily. "No, we go out for Belgian waffles on Saturdays. Boy, are you grumpy."

"On Saturdays," was it? As though Nadine's life had formed an unbreakable pattern after all of three weeks. Jealousy gnawed at Bernadette. She couldn't even say who she envied—Nadine, or Vince.

They started to walk. Nadine turned her collar up and put her gloveless hands in her pockets. "Speaking of grumpy, the other day Vince bet me I couldn't name all the Seven Dwarfs, and I did! I'm telling you, Bet, he was in awe." She gave her throaty chuckle that usually made Bernadette smile, too.

Not today. Bernadette could only shake her head in wonder. How could a girl whose favorite movie was the undubbed version of *Babette's Feast* settle for Vince Cirillo? Dwarfs! Try mental midgets!

Nadine bubbled on. "Vince has a thousand dollars riding on Wickham tomorrow, at three to one. Isn't that wild? It's for Anthony's college." She peered into Bernadette's face. "Something's wrong, isn't it. I'm sorry. I'll shut up."

"I was in Mr. Malory's apartment yesterday."

Nadine stopped dead on the path. "You *were*?" Then, "Oh, my God, *Bet*. Did he—" She gripped Bernadette's elbow and said fiercely, "Did he try something?"

Bernadette's laugh was part choke. "Yeah," she said, coughing, "yeah, you could say he tried something."

They tramped along the cinder path hunched into their jackets, sometimes walking backward into the wind, while Bernadette told all.

When she got to the bra part, Nadine whistled. When Mr. Malory came home unexpectedly, she squealed. "In the *closet*! Why didn't you just tell him why you were there?"

"I couldn't look him in the eye. You didn't see that bra, Nadine. It was like something out of a porn movie." Bernadette had never watched a porn movie, but she could imagine. With a vicious kick she sent a rock sailing into the muddy brown stream that ran below the path. "Anyway, he would have thought I was spying on him. So I hid."

"And spied on him." Nadine chortled in delight. "Excellent!"

She cried "Gena!" with the same startled suspicion Bernadette had felt. At the bathroom part, she groaned. "That is so gross. You must have been *dying*."

Truly, a great audience. With every sentence Bernadette's heart lightened.

When she revealed the contents of the binders, however, the sparkle died out of Nadine's face. The tips of her ears glowed red from the cold. Bernadette pulled off her own headband and made Nadine put it on.

They were at the gravel-filled square of exercise stations. Nadine collapsed onto a splintery sit-up bench. "He had our answer sheets?"

"Copies." Bernadette sat beside her. "He must have sent in the originals after he'd changed them. Probably kept the copies to see where we were weakest."

"What'd I really get?"

"Seventy-nine."

"That's not bad," Nadine said, before sinking back into gloom. "I can't believe it. Mr. *Malory*! He's so cool. Everyone . . . oh, hell." Suddenly she demanded, "What about Spic 'n' Span? You said she acted weird in her office, like she wondered if you *had* seen something suspicious. Remember? Is she in on this?"

Bernadette was impressed that Nadine recalled that. It seemed a million years ago. "I don't think so. She might have suspected him, just because Wickham had never won before, and he's the only one who could have done it, really." *Now* she saw that. "But she wouldn't have wanted to rock the boat. The worst she might have done was nothing. But as for being in on it? He wouldn't need her. He didn't need her to give him the right test answers. And he sure didn't need her help seducing Gena."

Nadine squeezed her arm. "Sorry," she said gruffly.

"It's okay."

Nadine chewed thoughtfully on her bottom lip. "So," she said eventually. "Now what do we do?"

"We get him fired." It was the worst thing Bernadette could think of, castration being beyond their power. "Maybe we could get him deported."

"What about tomorrow?"

"Forget tomorrow. Once we call Mrs.

Hamilton—" Bernadette looked at her watch. It was almost noon. "We should do that right away. They'll have to postpone it."

"You're going to get NCS to call off its Tenth Anniversary Bowl on a day's notice? You really think they'll believe you?"

Bernadette turned to her. Nadine had used the deceptively calm voice that made her debate opponents quake.

"Why not?" Bernadette asked warily. "I can prove I know the questions."

"Don't you think it'll leak out that Wickham cheated?"

"Not Wickham, Nadine, just Mr.—"

"Wickham is *us*." Nadine hissed it. Her black eyes blazed, and the pig earrings danced in fury. "It's the Wizards, it's our parents, it's the whole school. Everyone will say Wickham cheated its way into the Classics Bowl. Is that what you want?"

"Of course not. I'd give my eyeteeth to beat Pinehurst. *In a fair fight.*"

Nadine jumped off the bench. She grabbed one of the chin-up bars and hung there, her profile to Bernadette. "I'm going in there tomorrow like nothing happened."

"You can't. What if he stole *all* the questions? Just because I didn't see them doesn't mean he hasn't fed them to us. We're contaminated."

"*I* didn't cheat. And neither did you. Why

should we get punished because Malory's a crook?" She dropped to the ground. Bernadette could not help wondering how they had ever lost a debate with Nadine capable of such passion.

She swallowed. "Nadine. I realize it wasn't our idea. But it's still cheating."

"Is it? I say Malory didn't do anything worse than we do when we prep for a debate."

"What?"

"You know how we always take the desks by the window, so the sun's in the other team's eyes? And how we pump people in the hallways for clues about their cases and then take notes, in case we meet them in a later round? We'd read someone's case if they left it lying out and you know it."

"That's different."

"How?"

"That's their own dumb fault," Bernadette cried. She stood up into the wind, which must be what filled her eyes with water. "If they're that stupid they deserve it. We wouldn't break into their house and steal their files. We wouldn't sleep with the desk clerk to get the key to their hotel room."

"Oh, so there are *degrees* of honesty."

"I didn't say that." Though come to think of it, of course there were. "I'm saying Malory cheated."

"Bet, grow up!" Nadine's voice was full of scorn. "Who lied to your mother about how her car got scratched, hmmm? Driving around Mr.

Malory's parking lot trying to see where he lived?"

"That was just a fib. It doesn't mean I'm a liar."

Nadine pounced. "All right. If a fib doesn't make you a liar, then just knowing a cheater doesn't make us cheats!"

It felt illogical. Still, Bernadette's certainty cracked. They weren't supposed to debate each *other*. Desperately she cast about for some common ground, something that would put them back on the same side. "Nadine. What happened to Anna Karénina when she ran off with Vronsky?"

"That was Russia, ages ago. It was *fiction*."

"You told me she violated the moral code."

"Of *her* time—not ours."

"All right. But aren't some things wrong in any time?" Surely this was true. Surely some things were always wrong.

Nadine's face grew dark as the blood rushed to it. "This isn't one of those things."

"I think it is."

"Fine. Go throw yourself under a train," Nadine spat, and stomped off.

Bernadette sat back down again. She picked up some stones and chucked them at the metal slide on the nearby playground, pretending the slide was Vince. She'd thrown three handfuls when Nadine reappeared.

"Listen." Nadine sat down close beside Bernadette on the bench. Her husky voice was patient, as though she were speaking to someone who was a little slow. "Everyone is counting on us. Our parents, the kids at school. David, Anthony. Lori would be crushed."

Lori, who'd invited her father to watch her win something that took brains.

"It's not like he tried to get *us* to cheat," Nadine continued.

That was true, too. Though he'd probably been thinking less of their immortal souls than about the security risk to himself.

"It's the right thing to do, for everyone," Nadine urged.

There's always a right thing. Bernadette remembered someone saying that. What a dope, whoever it was. Nadine took Bernadette's unresisting hand between her own.

"Your hands are like ice," Bernadette said. "Are you saying all this because of Vince's bet?"

Nadine's "nah" was convincing. "Vince never bets what he can't afford to lose. He's not a chump." With shy pride, she said, "Vince thinks I'm brilliant."

"Of course he does! Compared to him you're Galileo! Aristotle! Tolkien!" Perhaps insulting Vince wasn't quite the right note. "Anyway, he's right. I think you're brilliant, too." Bernadette considered mentioning Anthony's "smart versus good memory" theory, but lacked the energy.

The cold grip on her hand tightened. "Whether I am or not, I want to show him that I—*we*—can win. The Wizards." Nadine had pulled the headband down low on her forehead so that the pig earrings were squashed against her cheeks. "Bet? Pinehurst doesn't need this like we do. There's no significant harm."

Ah, the shared language of debate.

"I won't answer any stolen questions," Bernadette said.

"Of course not."

"But the others will. They won't know he cheated. We could still win."

"So we win! So what!" Nadine thumped their clasped hands on her knee in exasperation. "If you hadn't freaked out in his apartment, no one would have known anything. This is partly your fault. You have to pretend yesterday didn't happen."

This dragged a laugh from Bernadette. What was a chump again? Someone who bet what they couldn't afford to lose?

She couldn't afford to lose Nadine.

She pulled her hand free and stood up to hang from the horizontal ladder. In Washington, some politician was either committing some horribly scandalous act or claiming he hadn't. Downtown in

Detroit, people would be shooting each other, selling drugs, sticking up 7-Elevens. Creighton itself harbored parents who hit their kids, and more than one house that never recycled a single milk carton.

Was one cheating teacher *so* terrible?

She dropped to the ground. "Let's just get through tomorrow."

Doubt and triumph battled in Nadine's face. "Fine." She jumped up. "How about a ride home?"

"Sure."

They started toward the parking lot. A few times Nadine seemed about to speak, but then she'd catch herself and give Bernadette a nervous little smile.

As they got in the car Bernadette caught a whiff of something foul. She checked her sneakers. In spite of her care she'd managed to tread in dog shit.

chapter twenty-one

I never seen anybody but lied, one time or another.
—Mark Twain, *The Adventures of Huckleberry Finn*

That night after dinner Joe Terrell went to the hardware store before it closed, and Martha settled down to clip coupons at the coffee table.

Loneliness drove Bernadette down to the living room. "Mom?"

"Mmm?"

"What would you do if you found out someone you knew had done . . . something wrong?"

The scissors paused. "Is this someone a friend, or just someone you know of?"

"A friend." A hero. A fake.

"*How* wrong?"

"Pretty bad. Something that would disappoint a lot of people."

Martha laid down the scissors and folded her hands in her lap. She cleared her throat. "Which people, would you say? Parents?"

"Oh, yeah." Mr. Malory charmed young and

old. "People who trust this person. Who think this person is very trustworthy."

"Did this person—is this a he or a she?"

"I can't say."

"Oh. Did they tell you about it?"

"No. They don't know I know."

"How *do* you know?"

"I heard something." And saw something.

Martha leaned forward and put her hand to her chin, resting her elbow on her knee. She had the air of someone who has waited a long time for just such an occasion. "Well, now. Let's think about this a minute. First of all, maybe you're wrong."

"I'm not wrong."

"Oh. Maybe you could . . . hmmm, you could . . . what *were* you thinking of doing?"

Bernadette picked up the scissors and cut the head off a man giving a seventy-five-cent discount on GLAD wrap. "I could tell some people. Who could stop this person from doing something worse."

"Something worse?"

"Oh, yeah. *Much* worse."

Martha's expression of acceptant, tolerant mother-daughter bonding faded. She sat back grim-faced. "Abortion is murder, Bernadette. You know that. If I have to I'll call Irene Walczak myself."

Bernadette gaped at her mother for what felt

like minutes. "Mom, for Pete's sake! Nadine's not pregnant!"

"She's not? Oh, God bless us. Is it—you?"

"NO. *Nobody's* pregnant. It's not about sex!" Though Bernadette could not help wondering, somewhat hysterically, who Martha would have guessed as the father.

"Oh, thank heavens for that. I'm sorry, sweetheart, but it certainly sounded—"

But Bernadette couldn't hear the rest for laughing. Suddenly it all struck her as exquisitely funny. Nobody cared about honesty; they were too busy worrying whether you'd been screwing around. Her mother moved over closer to her on the couch, which was a good thing, because even though everything was very funny, she couldn't stop breathing in shaky little gulps.

Martha hugged her. "Shhh, shhh," she murmured. "It's okay." She stroked Bernadette's hair. "Do you want to tell me about it?" She smelled warmly of soap and sense and safety.

Bernadette sniffled. She felt as fragile as tissue paper. "I guess," she said. The cat, the bra, the folder—haltingly, with covert glances at her mother, she told the story again. For once her mother didn't interrupt.

At the end, Martha pulled a Kleenex from her pocket and handed it to Bernadette. "I was in love once, too," she said, smoothing Bernadette's hair back from her forehead. "And I'm not talking about your father. Before him."

Bernadette did not think she had been in love with Mr. Malory—but she'd been wrong so often lately, maybe she was wrong about that, too. She blew her nose with a honk and snuggled against her mother's side.

"There was this boy who came into the café all the time." Her mother, Bernadette knew, had been a waitress in South Boston as a young girl. "He was at Harvard. Roger Vesterman III, but everyone called him Vesty. Oh, he was gorgeous. To die for, you'd probably say. Black wavy hair . . . and the clothes! None of that sloppy tie-dyed stuff for Vesty. He was from New York." Martha said "New York" in tones that left no doubt as to that city's sophistication.

"Vesty was always teasing me, asking what I'd study in college, as though my mother hadn't been a cleaning lady all those years after my dad died. Next thing you know he's leaving five- and ten-dollar bills under his coffee cup. Showing off, of course, but I went out with him anyway. We went to little restaurants in Harvard Square I'd never been in before but they turned out to be fun, when you were with someone who knew his way around. One time he got us front-row tickets to an Elton John concert."

"Didn't he do 'Rocket Man'?"

"Mm-huh." Martha started to sing. "Rocket

Man, doo de doo de something CARRY on—"

"And then what?" This was cozy. It had been years since her mother read her stories.

"And then I got to thinking that we'd get married and maybe I'd get to college after all—his family had money, I think they were in oil—until one night when he knocked his books off the table in the café and this picture falls out. It's a wedding dress from a bride magazine, and someone—a girl, you could tell—had written on it, 'What about this one?' His fiancée, no less. His hometown honey."

"No." Bernadette gasped. "What'd you do?"

"I dumped the coffeepot all over his senior thesis."

"You should have poured it in his lap."

"I wasn't thinking straight."

"Wow." Certain things became clearer. Bernadette would bet this had something to do with why her mother always wanted her to apply to the prestigious eastern schools—to outdo her old flame.

Martha squeezed her shoulders. "It's not impossible to be wrong about people you trust, is what I'm saying."

"I guess not." Bernadette took a breath. "You know, Mr. Malory never tried—he never made a move toward me, that way."

Martha clucked consolingly. "I'll bet he wanted to, sweetheart. A pretty girl like you, and so smart. But he'd be a fool to tamper with one of his students."

Thoughts of what he *had* tampered with brought them back to the dilemma at hand.

"What should I do?" Bernadette asked.

Her mother stood, the same martial light in her eye that must have scared the bejesus out of Roger Vesterman III. She strode about the living room, one arm crossed under her bosom supporting the other arm, her thumb under her chin, her lips pursed into her thoughtful trout face.

For the first time in hours, Bernadette dared to hope.

"Do? We do nothing."

Bernadette squinted. "Nothing?"

"You heard me. Nothing. Bernadette, I can't let you start a big scandal based on something you heard in your teacher's bedroom."

"His closet!"

"Bedroom, closet, who cares, you were in his *apartment*. Snooping through his bathroom, rooting around in his papers—how do you think that sounds? All Mr. Malory has to say is you're some lovesick girl who's been pestering him. They're not going to search his place, and even if they did, what do you think they'd find? You'd be a laughingstock." She sat back down on the couch and put her hands on Bernadette's shoulders, forcing Bernadette to look at her. "Sweetie, I can't let that happen."

"But that's—I wasn't—it would be a lie. . . ."

"It won't be *your* lie."

Something in Bernadette's conception of the world shifted. *Her mother was not honest.* It was as though scientists had announced that fresh air caused cancer. The betrayal by Nadine, who was her own age, after all, shrank to the minor blot of a venial sin.

She broke away from her mother's hold and struggled to frame a convincing argument, knowing as she spoke that it was futile. "Mom—to not tell someone would be like having company over for dinner and letting them eat a bad . . . a bad—crab!"

"That's ridiculous," Martha scoffed. "If someone had to get a bad crab I'd take it myself, and just pretend to eat it."

"What if *all* the crabs were bad?"

"Then we'd call out for pizza. Shellfish is always risky this far from the ocean. Now pay attention." Martha's tone became brisk. "If Wickham wins this thing tomorrow, then it wins. Don't ruin it for your team by telling them anything after the fact."

Bernadette tried one last time. "Dad would want me to do something. He hates when people cheat."

"Do *you* want to tell him? Because I just don't have the heart. But go on, go tell him the contest he's been bragging about all over the office is fixed."

Bernadette knew when she was beaten. Her mother would make a formidable debater. Opponents wouldn't know what hit them.

Martha moved over and took Bernadette's foot between her palms, massaging it with a firm, steady pressure. "Honey, you're exhausted. Look at you! First all that reading, then the excitement with Ms. K., and now this—anyone would be confused. But you're my daughter. I can't worry about Mr. Malory. My job is to look out for you." She kneaded both feet. She had very strong thumbs. "You sleep on all this tonight, and see if it doesn't make more sense in the morning."

She stood then, pulling Bernadette up to hug her. Ferociously Bernadette hugged her back, clinging to her mother as though she could protect her from the judgment of strangers.

"Good night, Mom. Thanks."

Martha kissed the top of her head. "That's what I'm here for, sweetie. Now scoot. Tomorrow's a big day."

Sleep took its time coming. Bernadette lay in her bed between freshly washed sheets, under the powerful beam of the new gooseneck lamp her mother had hoped would put less strain on her eyes. Surrounded by love. Drowsily she thought, *Just because people are wrong doesn't mean they don't love you.* She mulled this over awhile, and then tried the reverse. *Just because people love you doesn't mean they aren't wrong.*

The implications were terrifying.

Though Bernadette pretended it was not so, she knew there was a lot of Martha in her. If Bernadette was as tough-minded as, say, leather, it was because her mother was a stone wall. She had long ago rejected maternal taste in clothes, hair, books, and music. But notions of right and wrong—those were not questions of taste. She had learned right and wrong *from* her parents, and from the church they'd raised her in. No novel she'd read so far had shaken her faith in the Ten Commandments. Or, for that matter, in the Additional Commandments of Martha Terrell, retained more indelibly than anything Moses ever passed along. (Thou shalt not dawdle when told to do the dishes. Thou shalt realize that using the car is a privilege. Average-looking boys treat you better. Women can do anything men can do, but why would they want to?) One of the tenets of Bernadette's life had been that, in a pinch, her parents would bail her out. Well, she was in a pinch, and her mother had just thrown her a life preserver of stone.

She turned out the light. It felt too dark. She got up and opened her door a crack. Downstairs someone was unloading the dishwasher. Back in bed she stared at the wall. When this whole business was over she would look at things differently. Her mother. Herself. What had happened tonight wasn't the end of the world, she supposed. Or even the beginning of the end. But it was—Winston Churchill had known how to put things—the end of the beginning.

chapter twenty-two

Great contest follows, and much learned dust
Involves the combatants.
—William Cowper, *The Task*

The next morning saw the Terrells in their usual spot at St. Jerome's ten-thirty mass. In a lusty voice Martha sang "What Does the Lord Require" and didn't notice that Bernadette had maneuvered to have Joe sit between them in the pew. The Gospel was the one about Jesus making a blind man see; Bernadette listened closely, following along in the missalette. Maybe this was a sign. Until Friday *she* had been blind. Maybe the sermon would say what to do.

But no. The priest read a letter from the bishop about the importance of fund-raising for the new church addition. Her attention drifted. The Classics Bowl was five hours away.

Was there any way to get through it without cheating?

Only one way she could see. *Do nothing.* Nadine had said it, and so had Martha. Though she doubted they meant what she did.

The Bowl was about memory. Anthony had been right. Without Bernadette's memory the Wizards would certainly lose. Frank Malory would lose. That was good. Everyone else rooting for Wickham would lose, too. That was bad. The faces of Lori, Anthony, David, even Mrs. Standish, swam before her, but she pushed them away. She would not serve them a bad crab whether they wanted it or not.

You're deciding for them, the little voice in her head warned.

No, I'm deciding for myself, she told it as she rose to go up for communion. Mr. Malory had made his decision, her mother and Nadine made theirs; she would make her own.

"Body of Christ," said the priest.

"Amen," said Bernadette.

If any Wall Street analysts had doubts about the health of National Computing Systems stock, its international headquarters in Southfield would help lay them to rest.

The place smelled like money.

The Executive Briefing Center on the seventeenth floor was really a tiny gem of a theater, with seating for a hundred in tiers of squashy black leather armchairs. A raised stage held two rows of polished lecterns angled to face each other, flanking a larger, single stand for the moderator.

Above it all loomed a new electronic scoreboard that flashed and twinkled like a jukebox on speed. Bernadette eyed it with disfavor. It seemed more suited to Joe Louis Arena.

The room was packed. A buzz of anticipation made a wall of sound that threatened to shatter her resolution to do nothing. Her parents wished her one last "good luck," her mother's gaze loaded with meaning, before Bernadette escaped them and threaded her way toward her team.

Anthony's sport coat showed several inches of bony wrist and David's blazer overlapped his knuckles as though they'd grabbed each other's clothes by mistake. They were sticking close together and trying to look nonchalant.

Nadine's and Lori's pleated skirts and sweater vests coordinated too well to be an accident. Lori's bright hair was tucked into a demure knot, but her loose vest could not hide the figure that cheered stadium crowds every fall.

She saw Bernadette and gave a little yip. "I'm so nervous, I can't breathe. How about you?"

Bernadette mumbled something and avoided Nadine's eyes.

"Ah, Ms. Terrell. We knew you hadn't gotten cold feet."

Mr. Malory's slow smile, the teasing tone, were just as they'd always been. Bernadette forced herself to smile back as though he still controlled her heartstrings.

"I hear I have to thank you for fetching my cat on Friday." Mr. Malory motioned toward Ms. Kestenberg out in the audience.

Beside her, Nadine went very still.

Bernadette gave a modest shrug. It had been no trouble, she said, and his little cat was darling.

Just then his attention was caught by someone behind her. Bernadette turned.

A dark-haired woman, slightly built, thirtyish, wearing an elegant black suit Bernadette could fancy herself in, had paused in the doorway. Her brilliant smile at Mr. Malory made his look dim. She carried a clipboard and a palpable aura of feminine officialdom.

Probably had a bust of, say, 34B.

Bernadette gawked. Gena was nothing like she'd imagined. For one thing, she had clothes on. For another—

"She could be your aunt," Nadine breathed into her ear.

It was true. If they ever made a movie of Dr. Genevieve Fontaine's life, Bernadette Terrell could play her as a teenager. Gena had the same lean frame, the same pale, fine-grained complexion, the same straight, glossy brown hair. Gena's was cut in a gamine style Bernadette saw instantly would become her, too; and tortoiseshell glasses gave the chairwoman a look of sexy intelligence.

She even wore the besotted expression that, Bernadette realized, had been plastered across her own face every day this term. "Simpy," Anthony had called it. It was.

She forgot she and Nadine were at odds. "It's too bizarre," she murmured. "She trusts him. You can tell."

Nadine grunted without comment.

Mrs. Phoebe Hamilton swept onto the stage and rapped the microphone until it screeched. Her white hair stood out from her head like Albert Einstein's. She might be well into her sixties, walk with a slight limp, and have a tiny beige hearing aid peeking from one ear, but she was far from retiring. Those no-nonsense eyes made Bernadette glad she hadn't telephoned in the wee hours to tell this woman that her contest was rigged.

Everyone was directed to find a seat.

The little clumps split up as though at a wedding, Wickham supporters stage right, Pinehurst stage left. The Terrells snagged seats on the aisle with the Walczaks in the row behind them. Nearby sat Mrs. Besh, a.k.a. Miss Tanya, heavier and blonder than when she'd tried to teach Bernadette the steps to "Happy Little Clown." Bernadette wondered where Mr. Besh was, and whether he'd been brazen enough to bring his girlfriend. There was

Vince, looking clammier than Bernadette felt. He caught her eye and gave her a thumbs-up with one hand, the other hand holding a cell phone to his ear. What—oh, the bookie.

Ms. K. waved the arm without the cast. She must have driven with Spic 'n' Span, who gave Bernadette a bright nod and mouthed what looked like "kick butt." Behind them sat David's parents.

First Wickham, then Pinehurst, filed onto the stage.

The girls from Pinehurst were Madhu and Tanisha, the boys Aaron, Paul, and Glenn. Glenn Kim's name card bore the same captain's star as Bernadette's. She nodded to him—he'd cross-examined her from two feet away during a debate only a few months before—but his gaze swept over her as though she were a fleck in the carpet.

"What a jerk," she whispered to Nadine, and discovered that NCS used microphones of industrial strength. "Jerk" reverberated through the room.

Mrs. Hamilton gave her a stern look and began to introduce the NCS Research Committee. Four men, three women, none as young or attractive as their leader, Dr. Fontaine. Gena half-stood and made a slight bow. She sat beside Mr. Malory, Bernadette noticed. She wondered how they'd engineered that. Where were all the dirty minds when you needed them?

Mrs. Hamilton explained the rules.

There would be three regular rounds of thirty questions each. A Champion Round of another thirty. In the regular rounds, teams would select the categories. Six questions from five categories— three Open, for either team to try, and three Bonus, for the team that answered the previous Open question correctly. Wrong answers were deducted from a team's score. Opens were worth twenty points; Bonus, ten. Champion Round, twenty.

We know all this. Get on with it. Perspiration formed in little beads up high on Bernadette's forehead. Her heart thumped as though she was actually going to compete.

"Any questions?" Mrs. Hamilton surveyed both teams through gold-rimmed bifocals.

No. Let's go.

The world shrank to contain one white-haired woman, one cold, smooth buzzer, and the vaguely sensed presence of Nadine and Lori on either side. Mr. Malory, Bernadette's parents, the Channel 28 cameras—everything else vanished. This was all there was.

Wickham won the toss. Mrs. Hamilton looked inquiringly at them, waiting for them to choose the category. Bernadette remained mute. With a puzzled glance her way, Anthony finally spoke up. He picked Greeks, one of his Primary categories.

On the scoreboard, Greeks went from red to green and blinked off and on. It was distracting. Bernadette kept her eyes on Mrs. Hamilton's lips instead.

"What is the subject of Plato's *Symposium*?" the moderator asked in her rich contralto.

Every cell in her body urged Bernadette to respond, and as she fought her instincts she had a revelation that rocked her like a voice from heaven: *It wasn't cheating to answer questions they'd never heard.*

How could she have missed that? Stolen or not, if the questions hadn't been given to them already there was no unfair advantage. Even if *Malory* had seen them, she, Bernadette, had not, and therefore could not be held responsible. She only knew for sure that he'd stolen Romantic Poets. Fine—she would answer everything else.

This passed through her mind in less time than it took her to—*Bzzz.* "Love," she said, and cleared her throat.

Twenty points for Wickham. Beside her, Nadine exulted. *"Yes."*

Who stole fire, Hera's revenge on Arachne, Phaedra's crime in *Hippolytus*—the Wizards knew their Greeks. Watching the videotapes, Bernadette had noticed that early in each Bowl, contestants tended to pause a fraction of a second, as though verifying to themselves that, yes, they did know the answer. She did not pause. She rang in before Mrs.

Hamilton could lift her eyes from the card.

Anthony got the last Bonus: "What incident started the Trojan War?"

"Paris kidnapped Helen," he said, as though he'd hoped for something a little more challenging.

The Wickham side of the room erupted in applause.

The score was ninety to zero. No team—not even Pinehurst's legendary National Merit Scholar squad of 1997—had ever started off with such a bang.

Across the stage Glenn Kim's startled eyes met Bernadette's. She looked right through him but inside she was singing. Any thoughts of Mr. Malory were buried for the moment by the intense satisfaction of doing what she did best— competing.

The New Testament. Proverbs and Sayings. (Here Bernadette shone, helped by years of Martha-isms.) American Novels. Shakespeare. Pinehurst's Madhu called one of King Lear's daughters "Cornelia."

Anthony buzzed in. "Regan, Goneril, and Cordelia," he said politely. Plus twenty for Wickham, negative twenty for Pinehurst. Yes!

Mrs. Hamilton gave them a queenly smile.

Buzzing in, watching Pinehurst squirm, hearing Lori's whispered "Way to go"—sent adrenaline racing through Bernadette. It was as though she'd broken through to a new dimension, where all the good weapons belonged to her. They'd never heard these questions. You couldn't call this cheating.

At the end of Round One it was Wickham 250, Pinehurst 140. Pinehurst wore the same expression St. John's School for the Gifted had worn in the video: stunned.

"Bravo! That was wonderful." Mr. Malory joined them onstage during the break between rounds. "Team, what can I say? You were all magnificent."

His eyes were bright and excited, and for an instant the old thrill coursed through Bernadette at the way he said "team" while his smile spoke to her alone. Behind him Gena mooned over her clipboard. Bernadette flinched. It was like looking in a funhouse mirror.

In Round Two, David came in. Nadine punched Bernadette's arm as she went to sit out. "Nail 'em, Bet," she murmured with all the killer instinct any partner could want.

Nadine didn't have to worry. Bernadette's cheeks blazed. Her fingers yearned to press the buzzer over and over again; 290 points, wham! She hadn't touched *Of Mice and Men* since freshman year. *Blessed are the merciful, for they shall obtain mercy.* Bam! Take that, you purple punks.

Pinehurst must have been threatened with community college during the break, because they came back raring to buzz. Paul, the boy with chipmunk cheeks, chose the Restoration. He smirked at Bernadette as if to say, *Watch this*.

She leaned forward.

It was painful, but impressive. Paul knew who wrote *Mac Flecknoe*. He knew Christian was the hero of *The Pilgrim's Progress*. He and Aaron named Congreve characters as if they were old friends.

Bernadette wanted to howl. She knew all that, too, and if only she could have buzzed in she'd have proven it to the Channel 28 audience and the world. But now it was Pinehurst that had caught Mrs. Hamilton's rhythm. They couldn't seem to put a finger wrong.

Until . . . they choked on the Dryden poem describing the Popish Plot of 1678.

"Wickham?" Mrs. Hamilton asked.

There were no movies of Dryden. The Wizards looked to Bernadette.

"Absalom and Achitophel." She mangled the title so that it came out like an obscene sneeze, but Mrs. Hamilton nodded confirmation.

Boom! Another ten points.

Time speeded up. She couldn't spare a second for the scoreboard. Just buzz, get in, answer . . .

Maybe Mr. Malory had changed his mind . . . maybe he *couldn't* stoop so low . . . thank God I didn't tell anyone who mattered . . . *Bzzz*— "He shot a buffalo," twenty points, all right, let's beat the pants off these . . . "Sisyphus" . . . look at Anthony grinning, no one can say we don't deserve . . . get it, Nadine, it's Tennyson . . . Twinkie that, Glenn Kim . . . did they give you the ten thousand dollars up front or did they send it to your college . . . Grendel! Ha! Too bad, Madhu, let's try—*Bzzz*—"Grendel's mother" . . . oh, David, Becky Sharp, good for you . . . Aaron's a bum, that's three in a row he's missed . . . did you hear your daughter quote Whitman, Mr. Besh, you sneaky rat . . . *What* did the Green Knight almost cut off Gawain? She can't mean—oh, his head . . . that's all right, that's all right, we'll get the next one. . . .

The Wizards could win this thing.

After Round Three the score was Wickham 650, Pinehurst 590. There hadn't been a single question they had heard before.

The thin skin on Mrs. Hamilton's cheeks glowed, and her thoughts were easy to guess. What a pleasure to watch neatly dressed young people clawing over some decent books. Well, Bernadette thought, they'd tried to give her her money's worth.

Mrs. Hamilton announced a five-minute intermission. When they returned they would tackle the Champion Round, whose three judge-selected categories were even now blinking at them from the scoreboard like a cheer.

Romans!!!

Novels in Translation!!!

Romantic Poets!!!

Bernadette's gut muscles contracted. Romantic Poets?

Her eyes flew to where Mr. Malory leaned back in his chair, his legs crossed at the ankles, his hands making a steeple in front of his chin. His Wizards would now mow the weasely enemy down like the armies of Macduff.

He caught her eye, and winked.

chapter twenty-three

You'll find us rough, sir, but you'll find us ready.
—Charles Dickens, *David Copperfield*

"*I*'m not sitting out." Lori's shrill response to Bernadette's suggestion was attracting stares. "Romantic Poets are *mine*."

"All right, all right, hush up. What are Novels in Translation?"

"We called them World Literature." Mr. Malory had come up onstage. "Voltaire, Stendhal, Flaubert. Probably *Don Quixote*."

"More Russians?" Nadine asked.

"Probably. There's been no Dostoyevsky so far."

Nadine was Primary on Russians. "So I'm in. And Bet was Primary on World Lit."

"I did Romans," Anthony said.

David gave an airy "so be it" kind of wave. "Yell if you need a handsome face."

Bernadette said she absolutely had to use the ladies' room and didn't Nadine have to go, too.

In the hall she grabbed Nadine. "Did you see

him? He's counting the money. *These are the stolen questions.*"

Nadine's mouth set in a stubborn line. "I don't care. We *can* win, and we will."

"All right," Bernadette said.

Nadine's double-take would have been comical at any other time.

"It's our turn to choose," Bernadette explained. "If we can rack up a three-hundred-point lead before Romantic Poets, we'll have enough legitimate points to win. Lori can answer every stolen question she wants after that."

Nadine's face registered instant comprehension. But not conviction. "You want us to run up the score by more than what all of Romantic Poets is worth."

Bernadette nodded.

"What if we can't?"

"Then the game is up. We throw it. That's the deal."

"I'm not making any deal." Nadine moved in close and dug her fingers into Bernadette's arms. Her black eyes smoldered. "We're as good as Pinehurst. And you know it."

"Of course we are. Win *or* lose."

Light glinted off Nadine's glasses, hiding her eyes. "Only if we win."

BLATT. The buzzer sounded. Time for the Champion Round.

***

They took their places onstage. On Bernadette's right, Lori's golden book earrings jumped. "I'm so hot, I'm on fire," Lori whispered.

From the audience Martha called "Good luck!" Bernadette looked away. Her mother had had her chance. Bernadette was on her own.

"Give the Rabelais character whose name has come to mean 'huge.'"

In Ms. Kestenberg's library Rabelais lived directly above Sarah Sloan. *Bzzz.* "Gargantua," Bernadette said.

670 to 590.

Through *Madame Bovary*, through Proust, through *The Magic Mountain,* the Wizards built up their lead.

But Pinehurst could do more than sneer when pressed. And they were pressed. Bernadette felt their concentration flow in hostile waves across the stage as they nailed five in quick succession. Aaron was not such a bum when it came to Balzac and Camus. Probably read the damn things in French, Bernadette thought as he identified a minor character from *The Plague* with cocky assurance.

Then came "Name the protagonist in *Crime and Punishment,*" and Nadine—Nadine!—said, "Rasputin." Glenn Kim snickered and corrected her: "Raskolnikov."

Rasputin? What was she *thinking*? Bernadette gave her an incredulous look. Wrong guesses here would kill them.

Romans. "What Greek epic poem served as the model for Virgil's *Aeneid*?"

"The Odyssey," Pinehurst said. Anthony stared at his hand as if it belonged to someone else, then redeemed himself by answering three in a row. Pinehurst muffed two, Anthony recovered, and Wickham got a double whammy of net forty. He and Pinehurst split the rest.

Wickham 830, Pinehurst 670.

A one-hundred-and-sixty-point lead. Good. But not enough.

Pinehurst didn't know that, so Bernadette could understand Glenn Kim's murderous glare that made her resolve never to be alone with him without a very sharp pencil in her hand.

"And now for Romantic Poets," Mrs. Hamilton caroled.

OW! Bernadette clutched at her leg where a chunky black heel had just made brutal contact.

"No deal," Nadine muttered.

Bernadette smothered a whimper. A hole in her stocking framed a heel-shaped bruise.

Lori's sharp, perfect nails caressed the buzzer. "I'll get these," she warned. "I mean it."

Bernadette shrugged as though she'd never seen Lori throw a shot put. Still, she edged closer to Nadine, who would only stomp her to death.

Mrs. Hamilton took a sip from her water glass. "Name the author and the title of the poem from which these lines are taken:

"'She lived unknown, and few could know
When Lucy ceased to be;
But she is in her grave, and, oh,
The difference to me!'"

Lori swooped. "'She Dwelt Among the Untrodden Ways,' by William Wordsworth." A proud "Yay, Lori!" from Miss Tanya brought a sprinkling of laughter from the crowd.

850 to 670.

On Mr. Malory's far side, David's forehead wrinkled into furious thought. Bernadette could see the wheels turning—"Lucy ceased to be," haven't we heard that before?

"What is the work, and who is the author, of these lines: 'He prayeth best, who loveth best/All things both great and small; /For the dear God who loveth us,/He made and loveth all'?"

Bernadette beat Lori's buzzer by a millisecond. "Shelley, in his 'Ode to the West Wind.'"

Lori gurgled as though punched in the throat.

"Sorry. Pinehurst?"

"*The Rime of the Ancient Mariner,* by Coleridge," Glenn Kim answered. He did look like Uriah Heep.

"Name the title and author of the well-known poem which ends in these lines:

"'Beauty is truth, truth beauty,—that is all
Ye know on earth, and all ye need to know.'"

Bernadette buzzed and knocked Lori's elbow at the same time. "Keats? In his, um, 'Ode to a Nightingale'?"

A little *sss* sound came from Nadine, like the last lifeboat springing a leak. Mrs. Hamilton shook her head regretfully. This public school had seemed so promising. "Pinehurst?"

"Keats's 'Ode on a Grecian Urn,'" Paul said, adjusting his school tie.

Wickham 810, Pinehurst 710. Like a favorable tide, losing points for missing answers could carry the Wizards to where Bernadette wanted them with a very few questions. She'd have preferred to sprinkle her wrong answers among some of Wickham's right ones. But she was working alone, and there was no time to be subtle.

The audience shifted in their seats. Wickham's top scorer was losing her grip, and maybe the match.

Lori put a hand over her microphone. "Shut up or I'll kill you," she whispered.

"Name Shelley's lyrical drama in which an ancient champion of mankind is liberated."

Bzzz. "*Prometheus Unbound,*" Lori said, as though she hadn't just brought her full weight down on Bernadette's right foot. One of the smaller bones crunched. Lori seemed to lose her balance and put her hand down flat on Bernadette's podium to steady herself. Bernadette used her right hand— the left was massaging her toe—to shove Lori back to her own turf.

By now David was practically shooting off sparks. He tugged at the sleeve of Mr. Malory's new sport coat.

"In *Christabel,* Coleridge introduced a new poetic technique. Instead of counting the syllables in each line, what did he count?"

How could Lori not see what was happening? Bernadette pressed her buzzer hard enough to send it through the floor. Nothing.

From her left, a *bzzz.* "He counted the words," said a gravelly voice.

What?

So confident had Nadine sounded that Mrs. Hamilton double-checked her card. "No, I'm sorry. Pinehurst?"

"He counted the accents," Madhu corrected.

Now David and Mr. Malory were both waving wildly for a time-out. In mid-question, Mrs. Hamilton quelled them with a terrible look.

" —the 'sadder and a wiser man'?"

What the — Bernadette's buzzer would not budge. Pinehurst sneaked in with the answer before Lori could while Bernadette discovered a thin hook from a pierced earring wedged tight between her buzzer and its wooden frame.

Wickham 810, Pinehurst 750.

"What is described in this stanza:

"'They stretched in never-ending line
    Along the margin of a bay:
    Ten thousand saw I at a glance,
    Tossing their heads in sprightly dance'?"

Lori buzzed first. Everyone later agreed on that. But Nadine's deep voice drowned her out.

"Dwarfs!" she shouted.

"HEY!"

Mrs. Hamilton looked down her nose. "Once a team buzzes in, any team member may answer," she reminded Lori coldly. "Pinehurst?"

"Daffodils," Paul sang out, and sniggered. Dwarfs! That was a good one! Bernadette sent him a telepathic curse: May your new laptop electrocute you.

Time-out.

Mr. Malory was scowling at the stage. Bernadette didn't wait for him to decide who to replace. She headed for the stairs. At the bottom step her ankle somehow tangled with Anthony's foot—where had he come from?—and she tripped. People gasped, and only his hold on her arm saved her from falling.

"What's going on?" he muttered as he helped her up.

"Malory stole the questions," she whispered. "And Lori broke my buzzer." And my toe, she could have added. She leaned on him and limped, and then Mr. Malory and David were there and there was no chance to say more.

She left a seat between herself and Mr. Malory. Onstage, Anthony took her spot between the two girls and ignored David's tap on his shoulder. David shrugged and took the far end spot where Anthony had been. Bernadette's hopes dwindled. Anthony had the broken buzzer.

"Are we quite ready?" Mrs. Hamilton asked with impatience. They were breaking her flow.

"Several of William Blake's 'Songs of Innocence' have a contrary, or counterpart poem, in his later 'Songs of Experience.' What is the first line of the *contrary* of the poem that begins, 'Little Lamb, who made thee?'"

The buzz, when it came, was from Pinehurst, but the audience was diverted by a struggle on the Wickham side of the stage.

"It looked to me like the tall kid put his hand

over the redhead's buzzer," her father said later to Bernadette. "Then she kicked him. Or pinched him, maybe."

It was a kick. From the way Anthony clutched his lectern as though it might fly off, Bernadette got a good idea of where Lori's shoe had landed.

Mrs. Hamilton was turned toward Pinehurst with her hand cupped to one ear. With her other hand she adjusted her hearing aid, which emitted a thin, shrill whistle.

"'Tyger, Tyger, burning bright,'" Tanisha quoted.

"Yes, indeed." Mrs. Hamilton turned on her stool and looked at the scoreboard.

Wickham 790, Pinehurst 790.

"Goodness! Well, this is it, ladies and gentleman. Our last question. In the event of a tie, we will go to a tiebreaker of the judges' choosing," she said. "What is the name of Byron's travelogue in verse describing his travels through Europe?"

"Don Juan," Nadine yelled, at the precise instant Lori cried, *"Childe Harolde's Pilgrimage!"*

A tie, on the same *team?* Mrs. Hamilton turned toward her chairwoman of the Research Committee. Gena ran up onstage for a whispered consultation. Mrs. Hamilton nodded, and Gena handed her a sheet of paper from her clipboard.

"In the event a single team gives two answers simultaneously, the team is docked the points the question would have been worth," Mrs. Hamilton said, sublimely ignoring the menacing rumble that rose from the seats behind Bernadette. "However, since I did not make that rule explicit beforehand, in this case we will simply disregard the question."

Now the rumble came from the left side of the audience. Mrs. Hamilton ignored it, too. This was her Bowl, and she made the rules. "Our last question." She read from Gena's paper. "To whom does Browning refer in the following lines:

> "'We that had loved him so, followed him,
>   honoured him,
>   Lived in his mild and magnificent eye,
>   Learned his great language, caught his clear
>   accents,
>   Made him our pattern to live and to die!'"

Lori's face was outraged. Browning was not, strictly speaking, a Romantic Poet. She hadn't studied him.

Bzzz. With the faintest of sneers, Glenn Kim said, "He's talking about Wordsworth."

Or Frank Malory. Wordless communication passed between Bernadette and Nadine. They'd done it.

"That's *right*," Mrs. Hamilton said, excitement making her voice quaver. "That's absolutely right."

She addressed the audience. "Ladies and gentle-man, in quite the closest and, I must say, the best-prepared NCS Classics Bowl in our history, our winner today is Pinehurst Academy."

We had them beat. In the midst of deafening applause, Bernadette rose. Pride in her teammates made her step as light as a blown kiss as she ran up onstage.

The Wizards of Wickham. In her book they were winners.

chapter twenty-four

"Then over wine—a serious cabernet,
I think—the post mortem."
—Sarah Sloan, *Stacked*

The next twenty minutes were a rush of impressions. People laughing, taking pictures (Pinehurst). Looking like they'd gotten a telegram from the War Department (Wickham). Hugging (everyone).

The Wizards posed for an NCS photographer who snapped one shot before being yanked away to take a picture of Mrs. Hamilton with the winners.

Bernadette's parents. Joe Terrell gruffly proud and consoling, Martha sneaking glances at Bernadette while puffing out angry sighs. Bernadette was thankful it was so crowded, her mother wouldn't yell at her here. She put on a brave smile with a touch of self-blame. It didn't fool her mother, but it brought her father's arm around her in a comforting hug. She was *fine*, Bernadette insisted; no, she wasn't too upset, she must have drawn a blank up there, what kick? And of course she still wanted to go to the team dinner. . . .

And while she talked, her eyes scanned the crowd for her teammates.

There was Mrs. Walczak, wearing a face of long-suffering resignation at Vince's arm around Nadine, who was talking as fast and insistently as Bernadette.

A rusty-haired man with military posture had come up to Lori and Miss Tanya. The infamous Mr. Besh. So *that* was a lying cheat. It didn't show, but then — Bernadette's glance lit on Mr. Malory — in the best ones it never did. Miss Tanya's face went stiff, and Lori drew herself to her full height to look down on the skinny woman in black leather pants whose possessive arm was linked in her father's. Mr. Besh clapped Lori on the shoulder and pressed a bill — a fifty, it looked like — into her hands. Lori stared at it as if it held old gum. Then she threw it to the ground where the black leather woman covered it with her boot. Lori spat out something that didn't look like "thank you."

Ms. Kestenberg, cast held high, cut a determined lime-green swath through the crowd. Her becomingly flushed cheeks owed nothing to Revlon and everything to fury. She had heard Bernadette answer those questions correctly in practice and she looked ready to blow. Behind her came Mrs. Standish. Her face was harder to read. But definitely she did not appear as grateful as she'd been after the bee rescue. Bernadette had a bad feeling about this encounter. Whether Spic 'n' Span had helped Mr. Malory or not, she had certainly wanted Wickham to win. So had Martha. So had Ms. K. Bernadette didn't think she would hold up well under torture. All together or taking turns, these three could make an unholy fuss.

It seemed like a good time to leave. She excused herself to her father—"Got to find Mr. Malory see you at home I love you too"—and slipped away.

Talk surged and eddied around her.

"—don't tell *me* she didn't know—"

"—they were marvelous, weren't they? Thank you for your—"

"—Chocolate Macadamia Bread, it's a cinch and the house smells great—"

"—God, Leslie, she kicked him right in—"

"—the end of Thirteen Mile Road, and they won't be late, I'm—"

"—sexy or what? He can read *me* a bedtime story any night!"

This last, from a teenaged girl in green eye shadow and a miniscule tank top, made Bernadette just shake her head. Get in line, sister.

Mr. Malory glided from cluster to cluster like an attentive host, congratulating the families, saying he wouldn't trade his knowledge of the world's great literature for any computer no matter how advanced, and acting, in short, as though they *had* won. Bernadette dodged him, but she was awed. If he'd been born in America he could run for president.

"Nadine." Bernadette greeted Vince and pulled

her friend aside. "Let's beat it. Lori'll find us any minute."

"Is dinner still on?"

"Yeah. I heard him telling the boys about the restaurant. I'll meet you at the car."

The last thing she saw as the elevator doors closed was Nadine giving Vince a good-bye kiss that indicated a quality of research well up to her partner's usual standards.

Bernadette sighed. Of course she was glad for the things she *could* change, but she couldn't help wishing there were more of them. A gray-haired man with a Pinehurst Panthers button on his lapel watched her in the mirrored doors. At her sigh he gave a grunt of sympathy. "That was a very stimulating match, young lady. Well done."

Bernadette smiled tightly. Stimulating, oh yes. It took true discipline, but she did not snatch his video camera out of his hands and beat him over the head with it.

She must be maturing.

The second-floor table Mr. Malory had reserved commanded an excellent view of the front parking lot of Gordon's Grill. Bernadette and Nadine sipped the sparkling (nonalcoholic) wine that had been waiting in a silver bucket.

"Hey, Nadine?" Bernadette said.

Nadine raised her eyes from the menu.

"What made you change your mind?"

Nadine did not pretend she didn't know what Bernadette meant. She selected a bread stick and turned it around and around before she finally answered. Apology was written in every line of her face. "You did. To see you blow those questions . . . on purpose . . . in front of everyone . . ." She crumbled the bread stick into atomic particles. "It killed me. I couldn't let you do it by yourself. I mean, we're partners."

The wave of tenderness that washed over Bernadette temporarily robbed her of speech.

"My parents might sue you, though," Nadine continued. "For a couple of minutes there they were counting that ten grand like it was in the bank."

"Were they?" Bernadette asked anxiously. "How mad are they?"

"They'll get over it. When I tell them I want to major in Asian Studies they'll forget all about this."

"You *do*?" Bernadette tried not to sound hurt. This was news to her.

"Of course not—Korean is hard! Anyway, you know I want to be a TV reporter. No, I'll let them talk me out of it, and they'll feel like they had a close call." She grinned, and Bernadette grinned back. "I'll tell you *one* thing." Nadine wagged a new bread stick at her. "We could never have thrown the Bowl if he hadn't made us study so hard."

Which struck Bernadette, and a second later Nadine herself, as hilarious, in a sick sort of way.

They were still giggling when the boys arrived.

"Champagne!" David pulled the bottle out of the bucket and read the label. "For babies!"

"It's good. Here. To the Wizards." Nadine held up her glass.

"And the dwarfs!" Bernadette said.

"Would someone please tell me what happened back there?" David asked.

"Shhh! We're toasting," Anthony chided. He raised his glass. "We coulda been contenders," he said in his best Brando voice. "Instead of bums, which let's face it, is what Malory is."

David gulped his wine and fell into a fit of sneezing.

"There's Lori," Nadine said.

Below them on the pavement, long legs and a short skirt emerged from a little red car. The valet parkers jostled each other for the privilege of handing Lori her parking receipt.

"Did they do that for us?" Nadine asked Bernadette.

"Not that I noticed."

"Now, now. Don't be greedy," Anthony admonished. "You girls have a *subtle* beauty. It takes time to appreciate you."

"Years," David added.

Bernadette laughed. Maybe, just maybe,

Anthony's good mind wasn't wasted on a jerk. Her smile faded as she looked down at the sidewalk. "Lori won't wait that long. I think she's going to kill me."

The silence that met this seemed to indicate general agreement. David coughed delicately. "Well, she's sure going to ask questions. I will, too. I was there the whole time and I still couldn't tell you what happened."

"But you're so cute when you're confused." Nadine chucked him under the chin. "We don't mind that you're dumb."

"Hey!"

"Anthony started it! 'Subtle beauty,' my—"

Bernadette interrupted. "Look!"

Below them, the Porsche slid to a stop behind Lori and caused another scramble, this time for the car. Mr. Malory handed a bill to the attendant, who pocketed it and pointed to the back of the lot.

"In their dreams," Anthony said. They all watched while the Porsche cruised to the end of the lot where a brick latticework wall was under construction. Pallets of bricks waist-high were cordoned off by the kind of yellow DANGER—KEEP OUT tape that figured so often in Bernadette's favorite books. Mr. Malory maneuvered his car horizontally across two spaces.

Nothing was parked within rows of the spot. "He didn't need two spaces," Bernadette said.

"Sure he did," Anthony said. "Whatever Malory may be, that car is a work of art."

"Yeah," David echoed, but luckily Lori came in before they could get into an argument about cars, one of the few topics Bernadette did not feel confident discussing.

Lori turned heads in Gordon's Grill the same way she did in the Wickham cafeteria, but she seemed even less aware of it tonight. Temper showed in the flush on her cheeks and in the wild state of her hair, freed from its knot. Her blue eyes glittered with a fever that made Bernadette glad to see even Mr. Malory enter behind her.

"Hey, Lori, you lost an earring," David said. "What? What'd I say?"

Bernadette poured out some wine. Lori ignored it. "Well?" she demanded. "What's the story, Wizards? What happened back there?" She sat forward on her chair like a cougar about to strike. The glittery eyes zeroed in on Bernadette.

Tyger, Tyger, burning bright . . .

Mr. Malory said nothing. He pulled out a chair and sat down and then he, too, looked toward Bernadette. And waited. She should not have been able to smell the almond-spice scent of him. But she could, and it almost undid her. Some weak part of her craved his approval still.

Under the table, Nadine squeezed her hand.

chapter twenty-five

Anger is a short madness.

—Horace

The boys leaned forward. Lori drew lines on the tablecloth with the tip of a butter knife.

"Hid *where*?" David interrupted Bernadette's tale.

"In his closet. Pay attention," Nadine snapped.

"I saw you hide the papers in the binder," Bernadette told Mr. Malory. "I heard you talking to Gena on the phone."

The green eyes were politely curious, nothing more.

"What papers? Who's Gena? Why didn't anyone tell me?" David turned to Anthony. "Did you know?"

"No. Not for sure."

"Anthony Cirillo!" Bernadette forgot about Mr. Malory for a moment. "You mean to say you thought—"

"Shhh! Gena is Dr. Fontaine," Nadine told David. "That's who he kept visiting all month— there was no Gene."

"No Gene? You mean nobody died?" David seemed put out that his sympathy had been offered for no reason.

Lori had listened, dazed, her wide eyes fixed in disbelief on their teacher. That's how she must have looked when she heard about her father's girl-friend, Bernadette thought, and glanced away.

The waiter set Mr. Malory's Guinness down and discreetly vanished.

Mr. Malory rubbed his eyes. "Bernadette's right—I did try to make sure you won." He paused, clearly choosing his words. "You had all worked so very, very hard, you see."

He took a long swallow of a dark brown brew Bernadette wouldn't drink on a dare. "It started as a whim more than anything else. I thought, dammit to hell—Pinehurst makes it to these finals every year. Let *us* outscore *them* for once on that test. The brag-garts."

Anthony, Lori, and David registered fresh shock, realizing that they'd been cheated into the Bowl as well as out of it.

"Of course you caught it right away," Mr. Malory said casually to Bernadette.

Now the shocked faces turned to her. In the act of drinking, Bernadette choked. He made her sound like an accomplice. (*Weren't you? No! No, I believed him. I did.*)

"*We* didn't cheat." Nadine's deep voice was so

righteous, Bernadette might have dreamed their conversation in the park.

"Of course not." Mr. Malory seemed surprised. "To involve the students would have been unconscionable." He ignored the ripple of confusion that ran around the table. "And then the scores came back and we'd won the blasted thing, and I thought, so be it. Let's take them on." He took another drink. "Everything I knew about Pinehurst indicated you'd lose, of course."

"And if you'd been caught?" Anthony asked. "They'd have called us all cheaters. What then?"

"There was never the slightest risk of being caught," Mr. Malory said impatiently.

But no one believed him. He had just said he did it on a whim, and *that* rang true. He hadn't worried about consequences, or them, one bit.

"I thought it might be interesting to see what average American students could do if they were really pushed." His features lit with enthusiasm. "And good God, you pushed yourselves. Lucy and I couldn't get over it. You threw your hearts into it."

Five faces stared at him. So now they were "average."

"It was a rotten thing to do." David's fair skin was as pink as if the wine were double-proof instead of no stronger than Coke. "I read *The Sound and the Fury* in Cliff's Notes!"

Mr. Malory gave a patrician wave. "The best

way, trust me. Don't you see, none of you had a decent grounding. We had to play catch-up. My point is that you did catch up. You rose to the challenge like champions."

"Then why did you *keep* cheating?"

"Anthony, you were never meant to know." A mild look of reproach at Bernadette. "Once I'd landed you in the contest I owed you a respectable showing. I had no way of knowing just how strong Pinehurst might be. I simply—" He ran one hand through his wiry hair.

"Yes." Nadine spoke up. "Tell us about Dr. Fontaine."

"Ms. Walczak, that's personal," he said.

"Oh, please, call me Nadine. I feel like we're really getting to know each other." The froggy voice was sweetly venomous, and Bernadette stared at her partner with new respect. "You made up a dying friend so you could seduce the head judge—use her—and you're right, that's pretty darn personal."

For the first time, a trace of shame flickered in Mr. Malory's eyes. He'll never tell us, Bernadette thought. But after a long pull from his beer, he did.

"I called on Dr. Fontaine immediately after Wickham won the contest. She was very—pleasant. She made it clear she would see me, but only in her office during department hours. There were no private meetings at all, at first."

Bernadette wanted to shout, "Stop!" This wasn't

any of their business. Nadine put a warning hand on her arm.

Mr. Malory didn't notice. "I appealed to her American love of the underdog. Told her if Pinehurst kept winning that her contest applications would drop off to nothing. The NCS Bowl would become ridiculous, and Mrs. Hamilton's whole purpose in running the thing would be defeated."

It seemed to relieve him to describe his strategy, and Bernadette realized that for the last month he could have had no one to whom he could tell the truth. Even cheaters, evidently, needed someone to applaud their cleverness. You saw that in Sarah Sloan a lot.

"She lent me the Bowl videotapes. I pretended to be disturbed that so few minority writers were covered. A sad lack of diversity, surely, in our time? Anything to keep us talking. That put her on the defensive. She had often thought the same thing. The Bowl is privately funded, she said, and Mrs. Hamilton prefers classics she studied in her own college days. But now Gena felt she owed me something."

He caught the waiter's eye, and pointed to his glass.

"But the English department closed at five. To meet with her I had to leave school at three, yet I couldn't ease up on the practices. If I failed to get the questions beforehand, we'd need every scrap of preparation simply not to look foolish."

He seemed oblivious to the hostility around the table, but the vibrations almost swamped Bernadette. David sat as though watching a wreck in progress, while Anthony just shook his head. Nadine's grim mouth completely unnerved Bernadette. Lori had come out of her daze to stare at him with awful wonder.

The new beer arrived and half vanished in one long draft.

"You're quite right, David, that bit about Gene was melodramatic. But Lucy had to know why I wouldn't be at practice. And cancer has such good sympathy value. I called him Gene as a joke, you see. Lucy was delighted to help."

Because she respected you. He read Bernadette's expression accurately. "You were working so hard, all of you. I couldn't stand to see you lose to those arrogant snobs."

"That's bullshit," Anthony burst out. "You couldn't stand for *you* to lose. Because you tried for a job at Pinehurst and they turned you down."

Lori cut in. "But we *lost*!" she cried. No disclosures could alter this fact. "We could have won it, you said so. Everyone saw us lose, and my fa— everyone thinks we just didn't know enough."

"Lori—" Mr. Malory began.

"Stop it!" Lori's chin trembled, but her voice

was steady. And loud. Heads turned toward their table. "Stop talking. That's what you do, isn't it, you talk to people so they won't lose their nerve. You trick them into thinking they're smart when they're stupid, they're *so* stupid. . . . It was all lies—you didn't care about me. You didn't think I could have some kind of *power.* . . . I never did, did I?" She drew a ragged breath it hurt to hear. "You're just a cheat."

The cell phone bill. Bernadette felt a new kind of disgust for her teacher. *She* could survive this betrayal . . . but Lori . . .

Mr. Malory opened his mouth, but before he could speak, Lori picked up her wineglass and flung its contents full in his face. For a stunned second the only sound was that of sparkling Spumante dripping off Frank Malory's elegant, wet nose.

Lori shoved her chair back with such force, it tipped over. She stumbled out with every person in the dining room goggling after her.

David righted the chair. Mr. Malory mopped his face with a large linen napkin. The silence at the table stretched on until Bernadette had an irresistible urge to cough, sneeze, do anything to break it. Finally Anthony said, looking out the window, "There she goes."

Down below, Lori appeared on the sidewalk. A sprinkle of rain had begun, and the cars pulling up had their windshield wipers on. The valet parking attendant leaped up and produced Lori's keys as though he'd been waiting for her. She stopped him from setting off for her car. Instead she snatched the keys away and took off at a run while he stared blankly after her.

From one story above, the Wickham group watched in similar bemusement. How could she spot her car so fast, Bernadette wondered, and how can she run in those shoes? Because Lori, her small purse clutched in one hand like a track runner's baton, loped like a hunting cheetah across the parking lot. Her steady, driven rhythm set off a chant in Bernadette's head: *See Lori run. See Lori run fast.*

She passed row after row of cars glistening in the rain. Near the back of the lot, shiny yellow tape flapped wetly around the wall construction. Bernadette spied the little red Miata in a far corner. Lori almost passed Mr. Malory's car in its splendid isolation but then jerked to a halt. For one long moment she stood motionless, one hand on her hip as though she was thinking. The Porsche gleamed under the floodlights like a queen accepting homage.

Beside Bernadette, Anthony growled, "Uh-oh."

Brick stacks cast black shadows on the starkly lit ground. Lori dropped her purse, lifted a brick off the closest pallet, and tested its weight in her hand. Then, with a beautiful, powerful sidearm swing, she threw it.

The driver's window crumpled in a sheet of tiny cubes. The black square left behind reflected nothing.

Deep inside Bernadette something pulsed with a dark, terrible joy.

Lori reached for another brick.

"Jesus." Mr. Malory set his beer down. The glass missed the table, but by then he was halfway across the dining room. His students followed. Bernadette heard people crowding to the windows as she ran out.

"Did you see that girl?"

"Someone should stop her!"

"But that's a Porsche!" A bald man said this twice, as though he could understand attacking, say, a minivan, but *this* . . .

Out the dining room and down the steps they ran, under the canopy, across the drive into the lot. The drizzle had turned the asphalt slick. Bernadette's dress heels threatened to spill her at any instant. When Anthony grasped her elbow to give her support, she let him.

They reached the back wall.

The parking attendant had beaten them to the spot. Now he hung back, teetering in indecision. At their approach he turned in relief.

Lori was sprawled against the Porsche, her legs splayed out in front of her as though she were a Raggedy Ann doll. She still held a brick, and

Bernadette sympathized with the parking man's hesitation. No other windows were broken. She'd only thrown the one.

Mr. Malory crouched beside her. Gently he pried the brick out of the death grip formed by long fingers tipped with pale blue polish. With a groan Lori turned her face into his shoulder and started to cry. Mr. Malory patted her bright, wild hair while creases Bernadette had never noticed before appeared around his eyes and mouth. Into her mind came a vision of him years from now, comforting a child of his own.

"Man oh man oh man." The parking attendant had the tickled air of someone who's gotten a ringside seat. "She's lucky nobody got hurt."

When no one answered, he snapped his gum and tried again. "Guys think breaking up in a fancy restaurant is such a good idea, but some chicks don't take no for an answer, know what I mean?"

Bernadette eyed him with dislike. He was not her pal.

"Go away," she said firmly. She shook off Anthony's hand and crossed to Lori, tugging her to her feet. "Here." She straightened the crumpled collar, pulled down the vest. "Use this." Lori's fingers tightened around the plastic brush from Bernadette's purse.

Bernadette looked down. "Mr. Malory?" Her lust for revenge had died, replaced by an emotion so alien to anything she'd ever felt for him she couldn't put a name to it at first. It was pity. He had wasted so much. *Just because you loved someone didn't mean they deserved it.* Funny how that worked. She *had* loved him, she realized. Loved him with a hopeless, wordless ache she was sure she'd never feel again. All his knowledge! All the green-eyed charm, the approachable elegance, the way he'd taken his students seriously and convinced them they could do miracles—because *he* thought they could. God, she'd loved that. Some of that had been real, hadn't it? The way he'd taught them to trust in themselves—that was as real as the bits of glass under her shoes. Every single Wizard knew Wickham had outstudied Pinehurst. Every single Wizard (except for Lori at the moment) had learned that deserving a trophy was better, sometimes, than getting it. And he'd given Bernadette friends. Talk about the Power! Frank Malory had it, all right. Until he'd gone and wasted it.

"I'm sorry about your car. Will you—will it cost much to fix?" Will you call the police? Will you sue?

He got to his feet. Glass crunched. Raindrops glinted in his hair. She knew what brand of shampoo he used. His hand traced the line of the olive-green hood, and the gesture triggered another memory in her mind. Of a muscular arm polishing that same hood, on a cool, sunny day, while two girls worshiped from the highway.

He lifted his head. "Thank you, Bernadette. No, it won't cost much. I'm insured." He glanced at Lori's tense face, and then back to the car.

A wry smile twisted his mouth. She'd always liked his mouth. "Gena said I'd wreck it someday." He slapped the hood, and a last few cubes of glass tinkled to the ground. "And I did."

chapter twenty-six

Will you, won't you, will you, won't you,
will you join the dance?
—Lewis Carroll, *Alice's Adventures in Wonderland*

The next day at school they had a substitute English teacher who knew nothing about their regular teacher and who made them do a ditto package on structural grammar they'd never been taught. Ms. Kestenberg popped in midway through the hour. Mr. Malory had been called back to England very suddenly, she said, some kind of family emergency, and did anyone want a half-Siamese cat with a yowl like a tortured baby?

At lunch, by unspoken arrangement, the Wizards ate together. They decided that no one had to know about the cheating. Bernadette suggested this, with a look around the table that said the brick-throwing, too, did not deserve publicity. Mr. Malory would not file charges.

"Speaking of Malory—I'm not saying we should have gone along with him cheating or anything." David salted his rigatoni with close attention. "But ten thousand bucks! That's a lot of comic books."

"I know." A month ago Bernadette might have flattened him by saying correspondence school didn't cost much money. But David had worked as hard as anyone. And ten thousand dollars *was* a lot of money. She reached across the table and laid her hand on his, startling him considerably. "I couldn't think of any other way."

Under the table Nadine gave her a supportive kick and said, "No use crying over spilled milk. We can always enter next year. We know how to do it now."

"Yeah, no point beating a dead horse," Anthony said, "plus we'd come off as bigger whiners than Pinehurst."

David groaned. He'd never liked Proverbs and Sayings. "Yeah, yeah. A chicken in every pot. How long are we going to keep doing this?"

They avoided looking at Lori. Spic 'n' Span had announced that morning that the Wickham pompon squad had taken first place in the Governor's All-Star Championships over the weekend. Their school could now lay claim to the best cheerleading squad in Michigan, something they should all be proud of. She had not mentioned the Classics Bowl.

Almost no one had. Bernadette suspected it was from embarrassment, and didn't blame them. When she spotted Samantha's magenta hair coming toward her in the hall, she ducked down a stairwell.

Now Lori paused with a piece of pizza halfway

to her mouth. It must be a Red Day. "Hang on." Her eyes scrunched up with effort. "'The best-laid schemes o' mice an' men,/gang aft a-gley,'" she said in a distinctly Michigan-tinged Scottish burr. "Some people call Burns a pre-Romantic, but not me."

The other four clapped and made a fuss, and Lori's shy, proud smile went a long way toward restoring Bernadette's peace of mind.

When Bernadette got home, she found a notice on the porch that said flowers had been delivered in care of the neighbors. "Huh," she said, and went next door, where a woman with toddlers yelling in the background handed over the kind of long florist box roses came in.

"Enjoy them," she told Bernadette. She had a smear of peanut butter on her cheek. "Those days don't last long enough."

Bernadette thanked her nicely, while her heartbeat raced. Back in the kitchen, giddiness mounted in her as she opened the box. It *was* roses, a dozen long-stemmed red ones, velvety and fresh. American Beauties.

What else? She should have known he would not leave without telling her good-bye.

She rubbed her thumb over her own name on the card. The black handwriting was hurried and not done with a felt-tip fine point, but she would know it anywhere.

She filled the biggest vase she could find with warm water and sprinkled in the little bag of chemicals that came in the box. Then she sat down and admired the vibrant red glow that made the rest of the kitchen look dim. Finally she opened the card.

The black pen had written, "You are a winner to us, *no matter what*. Love, Mom and Dad."

Oh.

Bernadette stared at the flowers, then at the card, while chagrin as sharp as sand clogged her throat.

That was very sweet of her parents. Particularly of her mother, considering everything. And certainly no reason to feel like someone had just knocked the wind out of her.

Bernadette left the vase on the table. Moving as though carrying a brimming glass of something hot, she went up to her room and shut the door behind her.

She would never see him again.

On her quote-board every sentence spoke to her in his voice. Couldn't she read anymore without hearing that voice? That would be some legacy. If she couldn't read, she might as well be dead.

Sleep deprivation from the last few weeks hit her then like a blow to the head. She yawned hugely. Then she crawled into bed, pulled the comforter to her chin, and dropped into instant oblivion.

Her mother's knock woke her. For a moment Bernadette couldn't think where she was. She peered at her watch. Four twenty-seven.

Jeopardy! would be just coming on.

Two weeks later, Martha Terrell came down the stairs carrying a basket of dirty clothes. Bernadette was busy shoving the sleeper sofa against the wall of the living room.

"What do you call this when you write home?" Martha inquired.

"Lori and Nadine are coming over." Bernadette shoved again, and grunted. The sofa weighed a ton.

"Really. And would that be the same Lori Besh who's destined for cosmetology school?"

Bernadette sighed. "I was wrong, okay? A person does not have to like all the same books I do"—she gave another push, and the sofa scraped forward a foot—"to make a contribution."

"Amen to that. And what contribution are we letting Lori make today?" Martha cast a chilly eye on the area rug rolled up against the wall.

"She's giving me a dance lesson."

"A what?"

"Dance. Lesson. That's what they do at the junior prom." Her mother's mouth opened and stayed that way. "Anthony Cirillo," Bernadette added.

"Anthony! Well! Anthony! He seems like a nice boy."

"Eh. Just your usual clown." Bernadette's lifted shoulders suggested that Anthony Cirillo was no more remarkable than the dozens of boys always pestering her for dates, but what could you expect from Wickham High.

"When did all this happen?" Martha put down her basket and settled herself comfortably onto the couch.

"Last week. Vince told him about Kalamazoo, so he called to congratulate me."

Anthony's call had taken Bernadette by surprise. Yes, she told him, at the Kalamazoo Invitational Debate Tournament she and Nadine had finally defeated the Purple Peril. "After I realized we could have won the Classics Bowl, it was like I saw them in a different light. As humans," she said on the phone. It was easier to say serious things over the phone. "It was a psychological breakthrough." Glenn Kim's sneer hadn't bothered her, particularly since it turned to alarm as she and Nadine picked apart the Pinehurst plan in their most coordinated attack ever. Glenn and his partner lost by seven points. Courtesy of Twinkie and Friend.

Martha was beaming at her. Bernadette kept her voice flat and matter-of-fact. "So then he asked if I wanted to double with Nadine and Vince to the prom and I said, maybe. If there was nothing good on TV that night."

"You didn't say that."

"No. I said I'd go if he promised not to show me how he chewed his food."

Her mother's eyes gleamed, and Bernadette could sense her hand twitching to call Joe Terrell at his office. "Is Anthony coming for dance lessons, too?"

"Ha! He doesn't need them. When Nadine went to their cousin's wedding, she said Anthony was so good, he had girls standing in line to dance with him."

Martha bounced off the couch as if yanked from above. "Get up, get up! Here, you take that end."

When the room was as clear as they could get it without a moving van, they sat down on the couch to rest. Lori and Nadine were late. The faint hum of the fish tank filter sounded loud in the quiet, and the room felt strangely off-kilter, seen from this different perspective.

A cat appeared from nowhere and jumped onto Martha's lap. She rubbed behind its cream-colored ears. "I wish you'd talk to me," she said. She looked over at her daughter, and Bernadette realized her mother was not addressing the cat.

"I've *been* talking to you. I just told you all about the prom."

"You know what I mean. You've been treating me politely for weeks. I'm your mother, for Pete's sake."

"I know that, believe me."

"People make mistakes," Martha said with dignity. "Even when they act for the best."

Bernadette tried to coax Sheba to come to her, but the cat preferred her mother. "She likes you better," she said. "Traitor."

"I'm trying to tell you I'm sorry. About that advice I gave you." Martha's voice was tight with strain.

"It's okay, Mom."

"It's not okay. I don't apologize very often, so be still and listen. I didn't want you hurt and I thought keeping quiet was the safest thing. But your way was better." She gave Bernadette an exasperated yet admiring look. "It must've taken some nerve. Your father almost had a heart attack in his chair. He thought you were panicking. I said, oh no. That is the coolest kid you ever saw." Martha rubbed Sheba's ears and caused a rollover of feline ecstasy. "I was so mad I could've spit! But proud, too. I wanted to tell those Pinehurst parents not to act so cocky— that you threw it on purpose." She snorted. "They'd have believed that, wouldn't they?"

Bernadette kept still and listened and felt like Saul on the road to Damascus. Scales fell from her eyes with a clunk. So her mother had been wrong. So what? If love was a river, then Martha's was the Nile: enormous, life-giving, and at regular intervals capable of drowning you in murk for reasons you didn't understand. But you couldn't do without it. And no one expected you to.

She couldn't contain the wonder of it. "Just because people are wrong doesn't mean you shouldn't love them," she said. Then froze, afraid of how her mother might take that.

Luckily Martha followed her gaze, which was on Sheba, and assumed Bernadette was referring to the cat's owner. "I should hope not. You go ahead and remember him with love," she said, with the generosity of a parent who knew the male in question was three thousand miles away. "He did you kids a lot of good and I'll be the first to admit it. You *have* to love people even when they're wrong, sweetheart. Mothers couldn't manage any other way!"

Which put Bernadette in her place. But this time it was a place she wanted to be.

She scooted closer to pet Sheba's fur. Her fingers bumped Martha's. "Would you come to the mall with me? To pick out a dress?"

"Tonight?"

"Uh-huh. After dinner."

"You want me to?" Her mother's voice brightened. They had not shopped for clothes together since Bernadette had gotten her driver's license.

"I do." Bernadette amended that. "*If* you don't tell me the dresses make me look like a starving refugee."

"I wouldn't do that."

"Or say really loud that all we need here is a good padded bra."

"Never."

"*Or* tell the saleslady nothing ever hangs right on a girl who slumps?"

"But that's tr—all right, all right, I promise. We'll pretend you're an orphan. I'll be your guardian with the credit card." Martha smiled happily.

Bernadette smiled back. "And in case I didn't say so before—thanks for letting me keep Sheba."

Her mother waved a hand. "Don't mention it. She'll give your father and me someone to talk to while we watch TV, now that you're getting so busy." She got up, and so did the cat. "Maybe I'll just put a quick cake in the oven. Seeing how you girls can eat."

Bernadette grinned to herself, then lay back among the cushions with an old Sarah Sloan paperback she'd read at least three times. She didn't open it, however. When the doorbell rang she tossed the book behind the couch and jumped up to welcome her friends.

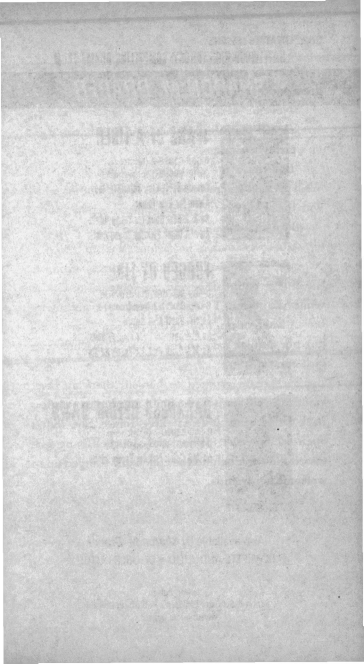

TEARS OF A TIGER

0-689-31878-2 (hardcover)
0-689-80698-1 (paperback)
**Coretta Scott King John Steptoe
Award for New Talent
An ALA Best Book for Young Adults
An ALA Quick Pick for Young Adults**

FORGED BY FIRE

0-689-80699-X (hardcover)
0-689-81851-3 (paperback)
**Coretta Scott King Award
An ALA Best Book for Young Adults
An ALA Quick Pick for Young Adults**

DARKNESS BEFORE DAWN

0-689-83080-7 (hardcover)
0-689-85134-0 (paperback)
An ALA Quick Pick for Young Adults

Also available by *Sharon M. Draper*
ROMIETTE AND JULIO • DOUBLE DUTCH

Simon Pulse
Simon & Schuster Children's Publishing Division
www.SimonSays.com

SIMON PULSE FICTION

Available now:

PAUL FLEISCHMAN

SEEK

The Life History of a Star

The
Queen of Everything

Deb Caletti

Sam's baby-sitting—
for good.

hanging
on to max